THE SIGNAL

The Bugging Out Series: Book Eight

NOAH MANN

© 2017 Noah Mann

ISBN-10: 1978356447
ISBN-13: 978-1978356443

Get action.
Seize the moment.
Man was never intended
to become an oyster.

Theodore Roosevelt

Part One

Numbered Days

One

Just in sight of the shore, cruising a thousand feet above the dark ocean with the aircraft carrier a hundred miles behind us, the smell of smoke began to fill the Cessna's cockpit.

"That can't be good," I said.

The instant the last word passed my lips and filtered through the microphone to Chris Beekman's headset, the engine began to sputter, cylinders firing in an asthmatically slowing rhythm.

"That's even worse," Beekman replied.

He focused on his instruments and adjusted the throttle, attempting to stabilize the aircraft's power. But whatever he tried, the response was as far from satisfactory as either of us had hoped.

"It smells electrical," I said.

As if to mark my suggestion as accurate, the sound in my headset fuzzed, then ceased with a soft pop that I could feel in my ears. I jerked the device off and saw Chris doing the same.

"It smells electrical," I repeated, loudly, speaking above the coughing engine.

"It is," Beekman confirmed. "The whole electrical system is failing."

Lights on the plane's dash flickered until, finally, the panel of instruments went dark. A few seconds later, the engine cut out with a final cough, the propeller free spinning for a few seconds before stilling, blades pointing straight up and down.

"We're a glider now," Beekman said as the nose began to tip forward. "A really crappy glider."

I looked out the windshield. The delineation between land and sea was plain, foaming whitecaps ending where sand and rock marked the beginning of dry earth. But that clarity in the darkness was not comforting. Not at all.

"We're not going to make it to shore, are we?"

"We're not," Beekman said, his hands tight on the yoke, trying to manage the delicate balance between putting the unpowered aircraft into a stall or nosing it into a fatal dive into the sea.

"How short are we going to be?" I asked.

Chris shook his head and focused on guiding the Cessna with a dead stick in his hands. He didn't know. Or maybe he just didn't want to tell me. In either case, we were going to be swimming.

If we survived the impact with the water.

I'd faced death more times than I wanted to count since the blight began its ruin of the planet. The possibility of my life ending had, since that marker in time, become an accepted part of my existence. Risks had to be taken to survive. Missions had to be undertaken for the greater good. Still, I almost laughed when I considered what was about to happen—I was about to be in a plane crash. Again.

Air Force One plummeting from the sky had nearly killed me and others from Bandon. Angela. Martin. Genesee. Carter Laws. That event was long enough in the past that it seemed just a distant memory now, not some visceral recollection. But those moments of falling to earth were resurfacing now as familiar twins to what I was witnessing through the windshield.

"As soon as we hit get your belt off," Beekman told me. "The first hit will be the worst."

"You've done this before?"

"You fly the bush long enough in Alaska and you'll have a bad day setting down on water," he answered.

The nose was tipping more now as the flat black swath of nothingness ahead grew larger. That was land, but we weren't going to make that. I wasn't even sure if Chris Beekman wanted to. Depending on where we'd approach the shore, we could be greeted with house-sized rocks rising from the sand. Those existed, too, just off the beach all along the coast both north and south of Bandon, though those jagged features seemed to be outlined by luminescing whitecaps smashing into their razor-sharp sides.

"Can you get us down between the rocks?" I asked.

"I'm not worried about the ones I can see down there," he said. "The ones just beneath the surface are what will tear us to shreds if we land on them."

"You're all good news," I said.

"Part of the scenic package," Beekman said. "Pilot narration of any crash for paying passengers."

"I rode for free," I reminded him, carrying on the attempt at a light mood.

"I guess I'll shut up, then."

He did right then as the controls of the Cessna grew heavier and less responsive. The churning ocean was rushing up at us. We were maybe five hundred feet above the whitecaps now.

Four hundred.

Three hundred.

"As soon as we hit, count to two and pop your door," Beekman directed. "Then get out of your seatbelt and swim."

Two hundred.

He put the Cessna into a tight left turn, heading north to line up parallel with the coast now off to our right.

One hundred.

The Cessna came out of the bank, wings level again and angled down toward the ocean.

"Hang on!"

There was nothing to hang on to. It was an instinctual warning that the pilot gave. And there was no time to do anything other than draw a breath as the nose of the Cessna, rising slightly as Beekman drew the yoke toward his gut, plunged into the rolling sea at the base of a wave, its curl lifting and tossing the aircraft. I had no time to count as Beekman had instructed. As the cabin heaved up and rolled, almost onto its side, I released my seatbelt and kicked the door on my side open.

"Get out!" Beekman shouted.

Water rushed in from both sides of the aircraft, washing immediately over me from head to toe. There was no need to fear that the Cessna would sink—it had already done so.

Of all the ways to die, drowning was my least favorite option.

There was something about the reality of having the life choked out of me by icy waters. I'd feared the possibility since I was a young boy. No incident had brought me to that feeling of dread. I'd swum in the ocean, across lakes, in rivers and pools, but always in the back of my mind was that nagging little warning that the soothing liquid which surrounded me could, in the blink of an eye, become the bringer of death.

Those very thoughts flashed briefly in my mind as I struggled to free myself from the aircraft's cramped cabin. The Cessna rolled to my side, door flapping in the swirling current. We could have been in ten feet of water or a hundred. Either was enough to end me if I couldn't get clear of the aircraft and swim up to air. With a surge of adrenalin, I heaved my upper body halfway through the door and planted my feet on the seat, pushing off to fully clear the now wrecked plane.

But I made no progress. Something was holding me back.

Holster...

The word popped fast into my thoughts. On my hip was the holster that held my Glock 30 inside my waistband, and the compact weapon protruding from it was hooked on the edge of the door frame. I tried to push my body backward a half a foot, but couldn't manage even an inch, the rolling ocean surf above creating a suction that was pulling me out now.

I was trapped.

What air remained in my lungs was burning to be released. But if I did that, I knew, it was likely I would instinctively take a panic breath, inhaling seawater. And that would be it.

A few seconds. That was all I had. I could already feel a darkness creeping in from the edges of my thoughts. The first hint of life fading.

Three seconds...

All I had left was brute force, or an attempt at it.

Two seconds...

I braced my feet and reached for solid holds on the door frame, fighting the swirling waters and the moving aircraft. That was when I felt it.

So simple a thing it was that my racing mind hadn't grasped the obvious manner of escape until my hand brushed against the cold metal of my belt buckle.

Buckle...

I abandoned forcing my way free and quickly undid the clasp holding my belt snug. As it released, the raging current whipped my body from the fuselage as the belt was jerked through its loops. Somewhere behind me in the dark water my Glock 30, still in its holster, was lost.

But I was saved. Maybe.

I kicked and swam up toward light that was barely discernable from the blackness, just an undulating sheen of dappled starlight filtered through the waves. The burning in my lungs clawed upward into my throat, to my mouth, and finally to my lips which could hold back the desire to breathe no more. They snapped open and I gulped.

A mix of air and seawater poured into my mouth as I broached the surface, a wave slamming me as I coughed the bitter liquid which had snuck in with the lifesaving breath. I fought to stay afloat, my eyes squinting against the stinging salt water, swimming and searching. For land. For Chris.

"Beekman!"

I yelled out to him, but the pilot who'd taken us to the ship, and who'd successfully ditched us near the shore, was nowhere to be heard. Or seen.

But something *was* out there. A light. More than one. Pinpricks of brightness in the direction the waves were moving. They were coming from shore.

"Hey!"

I yelled again, this time toward the lights as I tried to swim, but the current shifted and began to spin, trapping me in an eddy within sight of shore.

"Hey! Out he—"

"FLETCH!"

It was Chris Beekman's voice cutting me off, almost screaming in my ear, and by the time I turned toward him I felt hands on me, gripping my shirt and jerking me from the spot of ocean I'd become stuck in. He pulled me toward him, just a few feet.

But that scant distance saved my life.

I splashed onto my back, gaze cast upward at the wing of the Cessna rotating above and slapping down upon the water where I'd been like the fluke of some angry whale. The remains of the aircraft settled again and disappeared beneath the rolling waves.

"You all right?!" Beekman asked.

I nodded and spat more seawater from my mouth, breathing more necessary than speaking right then.

"We've gotta get out of this rip!" he shouted.

A riptide, or something approximating it, was pulling at us, countering any move we'd make toward shore. It threatened to whip us mercilessly in its current, as it was doing to the battered fuselage of the Cessna just below us.

"Lights on shore!" I told Beekman.

He looked and saw what I had, then shook his head.

"We'll never make it straight in," he said. "We've gotta swim parallel to the beach until we're free of this rip."

He stabbed his hand toward the south just above the water and pulled at me. I began to swim, following Beekman, arms windmilling through the chop and waterlogged boots flapping almost uselessly behind. Every few strokes I'd steal a glance past the rise and fall of the waves toward shore and see that the lights were still there.

But we were moving away from them as we swam south.

"It's weakening!" Beekman yelled back to me, turning his head only briefly to get the report out before facing forward again. "Start angling for shore."

He adjusted his course and I followed. Off to my right a patch of blackness drew my attention because I knew what it represented—one of the towering rocks that stabbed up from the ocean along the Oregon coast near Bandon. The monolith's shape was blotting out the stars behind, leaving only a silhouette to mark its position.

"Chris, rocks off to the right!"

He didn't acknowledge my warning. But if we didn't take a more aggressive turn toward the beach, the remnants of the rip current could very easily pull us right into the jagged seascape. We'd be shredded to bits if that happened.

I swam faster, moving my waterlogged limbs through the icy, churning water, until I was near enough that I could grab Beekman by the belt. He stopped and looked to me.

"Rocks!" I repeated, pointing toward the looming obstacle. "We've gotta head straight in!"

"It's still too strong!"

I shook my head. We had no choice. Up until that moment, on our entire journey out to the source of the signal and back from the carrier we'd found, Beekman had acted as leader. It was his plane that had carried us there. He was the pilot in command. Now, though, I had to step in.

"Stay with me!" I told him and turned toward the beach.

I immediately felt the pull of the riptide trying to suck me back out to sea. Still, I fought it, digging deep with each stroke of my arms and kicking with all my remaining strength. Beekman followed, slightly behind and to my right, the both of us making painfully slow progress. Even with the assistance of the waves rolling past us toward shore, it felt as though we were fighting a losing battle.

"Fletch, I'm losing it," Beekman said, his words spat through seawater.

I glanced back between strokes and saw that he was slowing to almost a standstill. The beach was within sight, the points of light off to our left somewhere up the shore. Just a dark expanse of sand marked our destination ahead. But without help, Beekman wasn't going to make it.

The fear creeping into my mind was that I wasn't, either.

"Come on," I said, reaching back and grabbing him.

"It's too strong," he told me.

He wasn't giving up—just stating a fact that neither of us could deny.

"Keep going!" I urged him, and myself.

It was hard to estimate how far dry land was ahead of us. Two hundred feet? One hundred? That distance felt insurmountable considering the inches it seemed we were progressing, if that much.

Pure adrenalin was fueling me now. And a desire to live. To see my family again.

Will...

That was what I thought: *Will yourself onto dry land.*

But it was not that simple. Desire, and guts, alone would not get either of us out of the churning ocean that was trying to swallow us.

"Keep...keep..."

In an instant it was as if something threw a switch within. All the energy that had powered me was suddenly gone. My legs turned heavy and my arms moved now only in a motion to keep me afloat, not to propel me toward shore. Beekman had drifted a few yards from me in the dark, but I could still see him, and realized that he, too, had reached a state of exhaustion which neither of us could overcome.

Slowly, the rip current began to draw us back out to sea.

"Fletch!"

The voice calling my name didn't belong to Beekman. But I knew it. I recognized it.

"Paul," I said, as loud as I could, the volume I could manage nowhere near a shout.

"Fletch!"

Before I saw Lieutenant Paul Lorenzen, I saw the light. Not one coming from shore, but closer, moving, its beam being washed in and out of visibility by cresting waves. It was a small flashlight, in his hand, sweeping back and forth until it finally locked onto me.

"Fletch, I see you!"

He swam right to me, pausing only to reach back and tug at a length of cordage that seemed to stretch out toward shore. It connected him to more rescuers, I realized.

Rescuers...

We absolutely needed rescuing.

We...

I wasn't alone, I remembered in a flash.

"Chris is over there," I said as Lorenzen reached me, stabbing my finger off to the right.

The lieutenant shifted his flashlight beam and found the pilot, bobbing a short distance away, treading water as the current spun him mercilessly.

"Hang on!"

I grabbed onto Lorenzen's collar and kicked as much as I could as he swam the few yards to where Beekman was fighting to stay above the water.

"Chris, we've got you," the lieutenant said.

The waterlogged pilot nodded weakly, a hint of anger in his gaze as he latched onto his rescuer.

"I'll hold onto you both," Lorenzen instructed. "And you hold onto me."

Our dual death grips on his stripped-down attire, tee shirt and shorts, it seemed, was answer enough for him. He paused and raised the flashlight above his head and flashed it repeatedly toward shore. A few seconds later a volley of gunfire sounded from the beach. Lorenzen tossed the flashlight into the waves and seized each of us with his now free hands.

"Just hang on tight," he said.

Within seconds I could feel it—movement. A steady pull on us. Strong hands were drawing us in from the ocean. Dragging us through steady currents and crashing waves until, finally, my boots dug into soggy sand beneath the water. This momentary battle to survive had been won.

Whether I'd be able to say that after we'd confronted what lay off the coast, I had no idea.

Two

"How did you get to us?" I asked.

"Lookout spotted you," Lorenzen said as he helped me up the beach. "They spotted your lights go out and called it in."

Lookouts...

Vestiges of our recent past. Volunteers scanning the roads and seas, and skies for threats. That precaution had been commonplace until the defeat of the Unified Government forces two years earlier. I'd thought that level of watchfulness which had been abandoned as unnecessary would continue as just a memory.

I was wrong. The appearance of the signal had made it necessary again. What the carrier offshore would force us to do was still an open question.

"Get me to a ride!"

It was Beekman barking the order as he pulled away from Enderson off to my right. I looked and saw him stomping up the beach, heading for a pickup with its lights blazing. Enderson looked to his superior and got a quick nod signaling the obvious—*do what he wants.*

"He's hot," Lorenzen said.

"Yeah," I concurred, knowing that Chris Beekman ran at two temperatures—ice cold and boiling. "He's just trying to understand this. Understand what we saw."

"What did you see out there, Fletch?"

I looked to Lorenzen and stopped on the sand.

"We've got company," I told him.

* * *

"A what?"

Schiavo had heard me. I knew that as I stood dripping in the town council's conference room. I'd been given a blanket and towels, and had shed my soaked boots and socks just inside the building's entrance.

"An aircraft carrier," I repeated. "Anchored out there."

She paused and looked to Martin, just the three of us in the room where momentous events had been discussed. Where fateful decisions had been made. We all were standing, each behind the chairs we might have sat in had this been some official gathering in times past. To mull over expanding the farming operation. To discuss contact with a newly discovered settlement. Mundane procedural obligations.

What I'd just brought into the room, though, was not that at all.

"One of ours," I said. "A big one. It's blacked out, with some kind of huge box on its deck."

"Box?" Martin pressed.

"As big as my house," I said. "We could make out cables coming from it and running down into the ship through one of the lowered aircraft elevators."

Schiavo was quiet for a moment, openly puzzling over the details I'd just shared. She wasn't unnerved or frightened in any way. It was simply her process of filtering through the information presented to mentally highlight the most salient bits.

When she spoke, though, it was not regarding the intelligence she'd been given. Instead she looked straight at me, her gaze softened without going soft. There was humanity in her eyes. Gratitude.

"Thank you for doing this, Fletch."

It would not be right to dismiss her appreciation. We'd been through enough for me to understand that she did not take lightly her place in asking others to face unknowns.

Especially when those unknowns turned dangerous. Or deadly.

"I'm glad we found what was out there," I told her.

"Except we don't know what that '*what*' is," Martin said.

"We will."

The assurance Schiavo offered was as much for herself as it was for us.

"Could you identify the carrier?" Martin asked. "It should have a big number on it."

I shook my head.

"It was dark, and, to be honest, I was a bit overwhelmed by the thing being there at all."

There was sound in the hallway and beyond. A door opening. Wheels spinning on tile, then carpet. A moment later Elaine rolled into the conference room, Westin following as far as the doorway a few seconds later.

"Are you all right?" Elaine asked me as she wheeled herself close.

I nodded and bent down, letting her hug me over the blankets and towels. After a few seconds she eased back and stared at me.

"What happened out there?"

It took a few minutes to bring her up to speed.

"It's not drifting," Elaine said.

Schiavo shook her head.

"At anchor," Martin confirmed.

"Two anchors," I added, recalling detail I hadn't shared before. "The chains entered the water at a shallow angle."

"That means someone wants it locked in that position," Martin said. "They dropped one anchor, then moved a bit before dropping the other and drawing them taut."

"It also means the same someones sailed it there," Elaine said, all of us knowing that was a statement of fact—not some theory.

"Sgt. Westin..."

The garrison's com expert looked to his commander and straightened slightly where he'd stood in the doorway.

"Ma'am?"

"That thing Fletch described on deck, with the cables running from it, are we looking at that as the source of the signal?"

It was an obvious question Schiavo was asking. I'd wondered the same thing as Chris Beekman piloted us away from the massive ship and back toward home. What we needed, though, and what Schiavo sought, was certainty.

"It would make sense," Westin said, falling short of the clarity he was being asked to provide. "There's only one way to be sure."

"And that is?" Schiavo pressed.

"Sever the cables," Westin answered. "If the signal stops, we'd know."

I'd thought as Chris Beekman turned us away from the carrier that we would, without a doubt, return to it. Some of us, at least. Westin's reply to his commander's question all but cemented the reason for doing so.

"Elaine's right," Schiavo said. "We won't be alone out there."

We...

Schiavo had very plainly marked herself as one of those to make the return trip. Those who would accompany her were yet to be decided. As were a few more important details.

"Just how are we going to get onboard?" I asked.

We...

It could be argued that I was using the term only generally, as it could for Schiavo's usage of the word. But she hadn't, and neither was I. She flashed a brief, thin, knowing smile at me. Once more, she and I would be facing an unknown together.

"I've shimmied up an anchor chain before," I said. "It's not exactly a sure thing."

I'd done so when sneaking aboard the *Groton Star* with Neil after the freighter, which had become Bandon's supermarket, was seized. That was a relatively short climb. Getting aboard a carrier would not be.

"I don't think they're designed for easy access from the water," Elaine said.

"Especially if someone doesn't want us to get aboard," Martin added.

Us...

Martin, too, had thrown in with the inevitable return to the carrier. If familial circumstances were different, and if a piece of shrapnel from a Unified Government tank shell hadn't severed her spine, I was certain that Elaine would add her name to the list of those ready to face whatever was to be found on the carrier.

"Fletch, did you see any sign of life?" Schiavo asked. "Any movements or light."

"To be honest, it looked like a ghost ship," I said.

The colonel thought for a moment. Chewing on the possibilities. And the resources at hand.

"Do we have any vessels that can make that sort of trip out to the carrier?" Schiavo asked Elaine.

My wife, who'd not only taken on the job of mayor, but had taken it with the utmost seriousness, had spent countless hours schooling herself in the town's capabilities. Everything from planted acreage to petroleum production. And the town's small but growing fishing fleet. Virtually every boat had been scuttled in the harbor when the population, en masse, had been taken to Skagway years ago. Since then, one by one, boats had been refloated, and repaired, and, most amazing of all, had found small success fishing the waters off the coast. Long ago a whale had been spotted blasting air from its blowhole, a joyous event in and of itself. But what lay beneath the waters, species which had, somehow, survived, were beginning to thrive again. As we were.

As we had been.

"I'd say Orville Pehrsson's boat is the most capable for an ocean voyage," Elaine answered.

"The *Blue Streak*," I said.

That was the name of Orville's fishing boat. An old, squat beast that he'd tended to long before the blight hit, and spent a full year restoring after it was brought up from the bottom of the harbor.

"Orville will do whatever we ask," Elaine said.

"I know," Schiavo said, though her agreement hinted little at satisfaction with the situation. "He's not the one I'm worried about."

She looked to me, and I knew what she was thinking. And who she was thinking about. Getting to the carrier on the *Blue Streak* was more than possible. Transferring from that craft to the larger boat on a likely choppy sea would be almost impossible.

Unless we had people already on the carrier to assist. To drop lines. Ropes to climb.

"It may not even be possible, Angela," I said.

"We have to ask him," she said.

The others caught on right then to what Schiavo was proposing.

"You want Beekman to try and land on that carrier?" Martin asked. "He just lost an aircraft. You think he's gonna risk the one he's got left to try that?"

"Navy pilots train for years to do what you're suggesting," Elaine said.

"We don't have years," Schiavo told her before setting her attention on me. "Where is he?"

"Last I saw him, Mo was driving him away from the beach," I said.

"Sgt. Enderson dropped him at the airport," Westin added.

"The airport?" Schiavo pressed.

"Yes, ma'am," Westin confirmed.

His house was close to the airport, but not adjacent. Why he'd wanted to be taken there, I had no idea.

"I'll talk to him this time," Schiavo said, looking to me.

"I wouldn't—"

"Fletch, his personal animosity doesn't matter anymore," she said, cutting me off. "We need him. This town needs him."

I shook my head, but not in disagreement with her sentiment.

"Not now, Angela," I said. "Later today. Give him some time. A little time. He needs to cool down after what just happened."

She considered my suggestion. It was already a new day, minus the coming light of the rising sun.

"He's right," Martin agreed. "Chris runs at extremes."

Martin had known the man longer than any of us. And had dealt with his moods and idiosyncrasies.

"Angela..."

Schiavo turned to my wife. The two women, the two leaders, just looked at each other for a moment.

"Everyone needs some rest," Elaine said. "It's been a rough night. The ship's not going anywhere. Clearer heads can deal with this later today."

She considered all that had been said, then let out a tired half chuckle as she looked to Westin.

"Sergeant, you want to pile on as well?"

Westin smiled and shook his head.

"Going against my commander has never been a wise move," he told her.

"Well, in this case you'd be right to do so," Schiavo said, then fixed on me again. "I'd appreciate it if you'd come along, Fletch. For a friendly face. But I'll do the talking this time."

That might be an unwise approach, but, in all honesty, I agreed with her at this juncture. Chris Beekman had to let the past go and put what was best for Bandon, and himself, ahead of all other considerations. That might mean fireworks, but, at the end of the day, he was going to do what needed to be done.

"I'll swing by and pick you up about noon," I told Schiavo.

"All right," she agreed. "I'll be at home."

I gave a quick nod and watched her and Martin leave together, the tension plain about her. She hated waiting to deal with a situation, even if doing so was both necessary and prudent.

"You two are going to need a ride," Westin said.

"Where's Hope?" I asked, noting our daughter's absence for the first time since my wife's arrival.

"We dropped her at Clay and Grace's on the way here," Elaine told me. "We can pick her up later in the morning."

Everything was moving forward, with relative smoothness, so that this new situation could be dealt with. Except...

"Thanks, Ed," I said. "Can you give us a minute?"

"Of course," he said, hesitating for just an instant before disappearing down the hallway and out the front door.

For a moment I said nothing. I didn't even look at my wife, my gaze fixed absently at the space where the sergeant had been.

"Eric..."

Her voice drew me out of the distance I'd let well up within. I took a chair and turned it to face Elaine, sitting and taking both of her hands in mine.

"Does this all feel right to you?" I asked.

She gave me a quizzical look, as if she was trying to decipher the subject of my question.

"Of course not," she answered. "That ship shouldn't be out—"

I shook my head, cutting her off.

"No, not just that," I said, searching for some way to convey what was just now troubling me. "The choreography of everything. The signal. The carrier. Our reaction. Doesn't it seem..."

"Seem what?" she prompted.

The gist of what had spurred my unease became clear right then. And it scared the hell out of me.

"Convenient," I said.

She let what I'd said hang between us for a moment, still attempting some understanding. But it wasn't reaching her.

"A threat appears, one that we can't ignore, and we react," I said. "We *go* to it."

"What should we do?"

The answer was both obvious and impossible, at least to me.

"Run," I said.

Elaine took a breath, one meant to calm me as much as give her a moment to gather her thoughts. She reached up and put a hand to my cheek, her touch warm against my still-chilled skin.

"You're exhausted," she told me. "And cold. Probably not far from hypothermic."

"I know," I said. "That doesn't mean I'm wrong."

"Sweetheart..."

"Elaine, why is that carrier off the coast? *Anchored* off the coast? *Our* coast?"

My cascade of questions elicited no response from her. Not because she couldn't offer any, but because she thought I was engaged in some cathartic release of stress.

She wasn't entirely wrong.

"The President sends his plane here," I said. "The Unified Government attacks us twice, right here. As far back as the Seattle Hordes throwing themselves at us, Bandon has been a place our enemies and our friends have known about. We're a target, Elaine. This place. This spot on the map."

She thought for a second, letting her hand ease away from my face.

"Maybe as long as we're here, someone, or something, is going to keep coming at us," I said.

"The entire town can't run," she said.

"Some of us did," I reminded her.

"A few dozen people relocating to Remote is not what you're talking about," she countered. "That's starting a new settlement, not..."

She stopped there, realizing, I knew, that she was engaged in a losing battle.

"You're not seriously suggesting this, right?"

"I'm just being open with you," I told her. "Maybe it is all exhaustion, or more. Maybe it is. But I am actually worried. Yesterday I wasn't, but today I am. People have thrown a lot at us. I'm afraid of what may come after this. I mean, come on—an aircraft carrier? Who are we to warrant something like that, unless we're still a threat to someone out there."

She didn't dispute what I'd just said. In fact, for the first time since I'd begun voicing my concern, I saw a glimmer of recognition in her gaze. A hint of acceptance.

My fear was now, in some small way, becoming her fear.

"Let's go home," she said.

I nodded and leaned forward from my chair and kissed her, then stood and pushed her out of the room and down the hallway. We would be home in ten minutes. Asleep in twenty. And in a few short hours we would wake again. To face this new test of our ability, and our will, to survive.

Three

"Excuse me, Sergeant?"

Westin nodded at Schiavo, reaffirming the statement he'd just made. He'd caught us both at the curb as she was about to climb into my pickup for the drive to the airport.

"Yes, ma'am. Another signal. Except..."

"Except what?" she pressed him.

"This one was brief," Westin answered. "An instantaneous burst of energy across the electromagnetic spectrum."

"Burst," I said, and the garrison's com expert nodded.

"How were you able to detect that with the jamming?" Schiavo asked.

"It briefly overpowered the signal that's shut down our com," Westin answered. "It originated on the same axis. In the same general direction. Southwest of us."

"Could it have come from the carrier?" I asked.

"Unlikely," Westin said. "It was...powerful."

Schiavo eyed the man for a few seconds.

"Sergeant, are you describing an explosion?"

"Ma'am, I don't know," Westin said. "The only kind of explosion to produce electromagnetic waves on this scale..."

"Nuclear," I said.

"I can't discount that," Westin agreed.

"But the jamming signal is still there, so it didn't come from the carrier," Schiavo said.

"My belief, ma'am, is that it originated far beyond the carrier."

"Can you determine how far?" Schiavo asked.

Westin shook his head.

"We just don't have that sort of equipment," he said. "And with the jamming..."

Schiavo nodded, ending the need for any further explanation.

"So someone nuked something," I said.

Schiavo had the ability to bring such a rain of fire down upon a target, and had shared the process to do so with me. Years had passed, though, since that responsibility had been passed to her from the President. Whether the sub that was tasked with listening for her call still existed as a viable weapons platform, or any sub for that matter, was an increasingly doubtful likelihood.

Someone, somewhere, though, had pressed the proverbial red button.

I thought right then about my family. Elaine. Hope. I was only able to spend a scant thirty minutes with our little girl after we'd picked her up an hour before from Grace and Clay's. She'd loved the sleepover with Krista and Brandon and baby Alice, her 'cousins' as we'd come to call them, along with Aunt Grace and Uncle Clay. This new world was like the old world in that way, I thought. Bonds were not always born of blood. Often, they came from shared experiences.

Surviving all that had come at us was paramount among those.

Now, as I set my thoughts of Elaine and Hope aside, another layer of uncertainty had been added to the situation we faced. Somewhere out there, in the vast ocean beyond the carrier, the greatest destructive power that mankind had conceived had been used. For what purpose, and against what target, if any, we didn't know. Not yet.

"Sergeant, have Lieutenant Lorenzen meet me at the Garrison HQ in two hours," Schiavo said.

"Yes, ma'am."

"Any other information, Sergeant?"

"No, ma'am."

Schiavo nodded and Westin returned to the Humvee he'd driven to his commander's house and drove off, disappearing around the corner.

"Duck and cover," Schiavo said. "The town's going to love this."

I hadn't said anything to Schiavo regarding what I'd shared with Elaine just hours before. My fear that we had become some perpetual target was even more unsettling now, considering what Westin had likely discovered.

But it was only a fear, I knew. An opinion. And I'd been wrong before. About Bandon in particular. At one point, not long after arriving, I'd thought the place incapable of advancing toward the state of thriving it had achieved. I'd considered leaving, striking out on my own. But I had not, and Bandon, and those who made up the fabric of its community, had proven me incorrect. Wildly incorrect.

Maybe what we faced a hundred plus miles off our coast was the last challenge. Maybe. We would be no target, then, going forward.

There's always hope...

Neil was right. He'd always been right. About that, at least.

I missed my friend.

"Martin's down at the harbor to talk with Orville," Schiavo said. "I imagine that conversation is going a lot better than what we're going to find at the airport."

"You're sure you want to take point on this?"

Schiavo nodded and reached for the passenger door of my pickup.

"No," she said. "But I have to."

Four

Schiavo and I arrived expecting to find Chris Beekman hot, like a fire stoked to its maximum. We did, but, that turned out to not be a bad thing.

"Chris," I said as we walked through the open side door of the hangar.

Beekman knelt on a small scaffold at the nose of his surviving Cessna, panels opened, tools resting on a rolling tray next to where he was working. He wore the same clothes from when I'd seen him last, trudging up the beach, soaked to the bone, shirt and pants now wrinkled after drying on his body.

"Kinda busy, Fletch," he said.

Schiavo stepped past me, intent on doing exactly what she'd said. For this moment, Chris Beekman was going to be her mission.

"Mr. Beekman," she said. "We need your help."

"I'd say that's an understatement," Beekman responded. "But me helping you is predicated on me making some modifications here, all right? So talking is the least helpful thing you can do right now."

Schiavo hesitated and looked to me, more surprised than put off. In her eyes I could see the question that was raging in her head right then—is he already thinking of heading back to the carrier?

"Chris," I said. "A minute. Please."

He paused and looked back, to both of us.

"You want to get back out there, right?"

"Right," I confirmed.

"And I'm guessing the reason would be to get some of you onto that carrier."

"You're already planning how to do it," Schiavo said.

He focused his attention on her. On the woman he did not hold in the highest regard. On the leader he believed had failed those she served. But in that instant of connection between them I did not see any of that old animus rise.

"I've been planning how to do it since Fletch and I were fished out of the ocean," Beekman said. "Planning and *doing*."

He nodded toward a collection of microwave oven doors piled on the floor, their glass portals broken and the fine mesh metal shielding within removed.

"If you want to get back out there, I need more of those," Beekman said.

"What are you doing?" I asked.

"Building a Faraday cage," Beekman said, jamming his hands into the engine compartment as he returned to working, riveting a piece of the metallic screen against the inside of the fuselage, adding it to a collection already there. "EMP brought us down. Well, not a true EMP, but the same results."

Electro Magnetic Pulse. The burst of crippling energy spat from nuclear detonations. For a moment I wondered if what Westin had detected could be the catalyst of an EMP attack. But where? Against what?

"There were enough Bunker Bobs up in Alaska when I flew the bush routes," Beekman said.

"Bunker what?" Schiavo asked.

Beekman kept working as he spoke, some determination driving him to complete what he'd begun.

"Bunker Bobs," he repeated. "Guys who'd move up to the big wide open and throw together some off-grid refuge because they wanted to be ready for some pandemic, or civil unrest, or—"

"A blight," Schiavo interjected.

"Nah. Most of them weren't thinking that plants would signal the apocalypse."

"Were any of us?" I asked.

Beekman ignored my question and continued working and explaining.

"The biggest thing they were all worried about was an EMP attack. From terrorists, or North Korea, or who knows. So I had a bit of an education hauling those guys in and out of their bug out spots. What an EMP attack would do. How it affects electronics. And how to maybe protect against it. With all this."

My rudimentary understanding of what a Faraday Cage did gave me some insight as to what he was attempting. If I remembered correctly, the metallic mesh was supposed to act as some sort of conductor to shield sensitive electronic components from electromagnetic interference. It was apparent he was trying, with his sole surviving aircraft, to protect those very systems which had failed on the Cessna he'd lost just hours earlier.

But I also recall hearing, on occasion, that such a cage would do little, if anything, against a true EMP burst. Then again, we weren't exactly facing that, a point which Beekman had already latched onto.

"That signal is powerful," he said. "Powerful enough to fry electronics if they're close enough for a long enough period of time. I can't think of any reason all those systems on an aircraft would fail, and fail spectacularly, without something affecting them."

Schiavo approached the nose of the Cessna and stepped onto the small scaffolding next to Beekman, peering past him into the engine compartment.

"This will protect the plane?" she asked.

Beekman hesitated just an instant, likely, I thought, because he'd expected the discord which had existed between them to simmer still on her end. But she was letting it go, as was he. At least for now.

"We'll know in due time," he said.

"Chris..."

He paused his work and turned toward me.

"Can you land on that carrier?"

He only considered my question for a few seconds, as he'd obviously already considered the necessity of that very act.

"Probably," he said.

"That's not promising," Schiavo commented.

"I'm cocky," Beekman said. "I know that. But not above my ability. If I can't do something, I admit it. This thing that you want to do...it's a maybe."

"Can you take off again after landing?" Schiavo asked.

Beekman nodded.

"I'm more confident of that. But there's a lot of variables. How much weight on both legs of the trip."

"Three passengers with gear," she told him.

"Three passengers with only *essential* gear," he said.

"The plan is to bring any heavy stuff out by boat," I said. "With more personnel."

"Getting us on the carrier will allow us to board everyone from the boat," Schiavo added.

"Everyone," Beekman repeated, though he didn't react negatively to what he'd heard. "I have a feeling you may need them."

He set his tools aside and stepped off the scaffolding and began picking through the microwave doors.

"No reason for that thing to be out there other than to hurt us," he said.

Without stating so explicitly, Beekman had agreed with the concerns I'd expressed to Elaine. And if he was worried...

"If I get some help to scavenge more of these doors, can you be ready to fly tomorrow afternoon?" Schiavo asked.

"Get me enough and I'll be ready tonight," Beekman answered.

"Tomorrow will be good," I said.

Beekman returned to the engine compartment with another piece of wire mesh. We turned to leave. At least I thought we had. Schiavo, instead, simply stepped off the scaffolding and stood there, close to the man working to keep his plane safe against the unseen threat blasting through the air as we'd spoken.

"Beekman..."

Beekman stopped and looked to Schiavo.

"I need you to get us there," she said. "We can come back on the boat, but I need to know you can get us on that ship in one piece."

"You don't want a maybe," he said.

"I don't."

He considered the choice being presented to him. Commit to success, or there was every chance Schiavo would scrub the plan. Risks were one thing in her business. The chance of dying was ever-present. But risks had to be calculated. Death had to be a possibility—not a likelihood.

"I can land on it," Beekman said. "I can get you there. It may not be pretty, but I'll get you there in one piece."

Schiavo accepted that with a nodding hint of a smile.

"Okay," she said, pleased. "Fair enough."

Five

"I was thinking about what you said."

Elaine looked at me from across the dinner table, waiting for me to respond. Just to my right, Hope was playing with a pile of peas on her plate, the high chair struggling to contain the bundle of two-year-old energy that she was.

"And?"

"What would you do?" my wife asked.

What would I do? If I were an omnipotent being, it might be the smart play to turn back the clock to the point before the blight was even a glint in some scientist's eye and prevent it from ever happening. But, with that power, I would effectively erase what I saw before me at our modest kitchen table. Elaine would still be FBI Special Agent Elaine Morales, working white collar crime in some anonymous Bureau building somewhere. And Hope...

Our child would not be at all. No part of her would cross our separated minds. This future we'd come to know, and to embrace, would not even exist in a fevered dream.

Elaine did not seek some fanciful explanation of the fears I'd expressed, but the reality of the life I did now have was, to me, as inconceivable as it was real. I'd never dreamed of what I now had, and what I would do to protect it, to protect them, knew no bounds.

"Where would you want to go?" she pressed me when my silence lingered.

"Moving a town isn't an easy thing to do," I said.

"No," she said, shaking her head slightly. "Not the town. You. Us."

"Us?"

"A small group," she said. "Like they did setting up Remote."

That settlement had been born of dissatisfaction with the town's leadership. Forty plus individuals had rebuilt the tiny hamlet decimated by the blight. Why, though, was Elaine suggesting what I thought she was?

"Wait," I said, openly confused. "I was talking about the town, Elaine. Everyone."

"I know," she said. "But we'd have to think of our part in a smaller group."

I sat back in my chair and stared at her for a moment.

"What if you're right?" she asked. "And we do have a target on us. Up and moving everyone, would that make us safe? Or would the target always be on us?"

"I don't know," I said.

"One basket, all the eggs," she said, drawing on a metaphor to succinctly describe our situation.

"What are you saying, Elaine?" I asked, turning the query back on her.

My wife reached to our daughter and tapped the plate, signaling that it was time she start eating and stop playing. Hope obliged, awkwardly spooning peas into her mouth.

"Once this thing with the carrier is in the past, I'm thinking of bringing up with the council that we break up Bandon. We divide into eight, maybe ten groups, and spread out. Not close, either. Far enough that each group would have to work to survive on their own. True independence."

If I'd been able to lean back against my chair anymore, it would have toppled. That I had planted such a thought in my wife's head was not even a possibility when I'd told her of my fears. Fears that might have been symptoms of exhaustion and hypothermia.

She, though, had been astute enough to recognize that they weren't.

"What do you think?" she asked.

I took in the sight of her. The woman I'd not even known when the blight rolled over the planet. The woman who'd traveled with me, suffered with me, and fallen for me. The woman who'd sacrificed the use of her legs to protect her adopted hometown.

A place that she now was concluding had served its purpose.

"You can't force people to go," I told her.

"I know," she said. "But you can lead them."

In those words, and in the look that accompanied them, I could see that our time in Bandon, no matter what happened aboard the carrier, was drawing to a close.

Six

There was no fanfare. Our mission to the carrier, both parts, began ten hours apart, with the *Blue Streak* departing Bandon's harbor before seven in the morning on a journey which Orville Pehrsson estimated would take twelve hours across open ocean. That marker in time informed our departure from the airfield. We needed to reach our destination with the last light of day almost gone. Darkness would be our shield.

But it was also going to be our nemesis.

"A night landing," Elaine said as I gave my gear a last look.

"Night-ish," I corrected her.

"Chris assured her he can do this, Angela said."

"Yeah," I confirmed.

"You don't sound convinced," she said.

"I wouldn't say he was backed into a corner, but it wasn't far from that."

She shifted her attention, trying not to focus on that most difficult of tasks, and let herself appraise the gear I was readying instead.

"Four mags?" she asked, uncertain about the choice that was not a choice.

"Ammunition is weight," I said. "Weight wastes fuel. And, as Chris put it, we don't want to land a fat Cessna on a moving airstrip."

"I guess that makes sense," she said.

"He knows what he's doing," I reassured her.

"I know that."

I finished stowing my equipment in the small backpack and slipped the four thirty-round magazines of 5.56 ammo into the snug gear vest I wore. Besides that I had one full mag in my AR, two spare mags for my Springfield, a knife on my belt, and a compact five shot Smith & Wesson .357 magnum revolver in a boot holster on the inside of my left leg. Martin and Angela were similarly outfitted. Chris Beekman, whose only job once aboard was to keep his plane in one piece, was bringing a sawed-off 12-gauge Mossberg room broom, with a pistol grip and no stock. It was a hideously inaccurate shotgun, but the man who would be piloting us to the carrier insisted that the pattern it put out would make up for his innate inability to hit the proverbial side of a barn.

"Fletch..."

It was Schiavo. She was standing just under the Cessna's right wingtip. Beyond her, Martin was already aboard in one of the rear seats. Just in front of him, Beekman sat at the controls, waiting for the go ahead to start the engine.

"Gotta go," I said to my wife, leaning to kiss her.

But as I tried to pull back she put her arms around my neck and held me there, kissing me longer. When she was finally done she let me ease back a little and looked me straight in the eye.

"Your little girl is going to want to see you again," she said. "Make that happen."

I smiled and nodded.

"I can't resist that order," I said.

She released me and I stood, hauling my small backpack toward the plane. The baggage door just aft of the rear seats was open, Martin's small bag already inside. Schiavo and I placed ours, each containing only the necessities—rope, an emergency supply of food and water, a medical kit, and extra lights and batteries.

"Start it up, Beekman," Schiavo said as she secured the baggage door.

The propeller jerked, the engine growling for a moment before catching, prop spinning up to speed. Schiavo climbed in past the tipped front seat and took the space next to her husband. I readied the front passenger seat and slipped in, closing the door and donning my headset, as the others already had.

"Ban—" Beekman chuckled and looked to me. "I almost called in our departure."

Doing so would have been pointless. The airwaves were still choked with the signal which had overpowered every wireless transmission.

"Let's just get airborne then, I guess," he said, and revved the throttles.

I glanced out the window, to my wife. Lt. Lorenzen was standing behind, waiting to drive her back to town. She raised her hand in a brief, almost bittersweet wave, and I pressed my palm against the glass, returning the gesture as best I could. As the Cessna accelerated and turned off the taxiway I lost sight of her. Beekman swung the plane into a fast ninety-degree turn at the beginning of the runway and firewalled the throttles, wasting no time.

"We're on the clock," the pilot said as the nose rose gently off the ground.

An hour flight out there, give or take. That was what we had ahead of us. Then, if all went as planned, we would land. On a pitching deck. With an obstacle the size of a house halfway down the runway. Those who'd set out before us, Westin, Hart, and Laws aboard Orville's fishing boat, would be just an hour or so away from the carrier. Fifteen miles from it. With the sun setting behind it, if the weather was clear, they should be able to see its silhouette by now.

Meaning they could be seen as well.

There was some stealth to this operation, but none of us was under any illusion that we were being covert by any stretch of the imagination. The mere act of slamming a multi-ton aircraft onto the ship's deck would be enough to announce or presence.

But we had to get there. *Had* to. There was some reason, some unknown purpose, to the carrier appearing off our coast blasting a jamming signal. And all of us knew that benign explanations for what we'd discovered would be pure fantasy. Nothing good would be found out there. I felt that in my gut.

"Fletch..."

It was Schiavo, talking through the intercom as the Cessna climbed into the darkening day.

"What?"

"Do you remember?"

The question was vague. So vague that I knew exactly what she was talking about. I turned halfway around in my seat and looked Schiavo square in the eye.

"I do," I said.

Viper Diamond Nine...

The call sign for the sub which would unleash nuclear hell at her command, or mine, assuming it still existed. That she was bringing this up hinted to me that she saw using that awesome power to obliterate the carrier, if that became necessary. A hundred and thirty miles out at sea, any effect on Bandon would be almost nonexistent. There was one very large problem with this possible scenario.

The sub would be as unreachable as someone standing fifty feet away with a walkie talkie. No transmissions were getting anywhere.

"Job number one when my guys board from the *Blue Streak* is shutting that signal down," Schiavo said. "Then we can figure out why the damn thing is there in the first place."

I nodded and faced forward again.

"You guys keeping secrets from me?" Beekman asked over the intercom. "That's not nice."

"You don't want to know," I told him.

"You sound pretty sure about that, Fletch."

"I am."

"Why?" he pressed.

Knowledge was power. But it could also be a curse.

"Because I wish that I didn't know."

Part Two

The Carrier

Seven

There was no protocol for what Beekman was attempting. With light fading in the west, only a thin blue glow on the watery horizon, he had just enough definition in the carrier's shape to allow some semblance of a normal approach to the flight deck—as normal as one could term what he was doing. There was no training for putting a small civilian aircraft down on the moving deck of the craft which was used to recovering supersonic jets with sophisticated guidance and arresting cables to prevent them from rocketing off the maritime landing strip and into the sea.

Another issue, though, also troubled me as we approached the massive vessel.

"Still no sign of the *Blue Streak*," I said, glancing back toward Martin and Schiavo.

We'd crossed more than a hundred miles of open ocean, following the same course that the fishing vessel carrying the remainder of our team would be, but none of us had seen any trace of them. No boat bobbing on the water. No wake tracing the route of their travel.

"Doesn't mean anything," Beekman said as he maneuvered the Cessna for as straight an approach as possible. "We ran through several patches of clouds. Any one of those could have masked their position."

"But they should be in the area by now," I said. "If—"

"If they were able to run at top speed," Beekman interjected, offering a dose of reality to counter my concern.

"If the sea wasn't rougher than expected. There's a lot of variables, and I'd be happy to lay them all out for you, but right now I'd really like you to clam up so I can make this happen."

He never looked at me as he offered the rebuke. It was deserved, I supposed. Seeing or not seeing the *Blue Streak* mattered not at all if we weren't able to make a safe landing.

"Be ready," Beekman cautioned us. "I'm going to brake hard as soon as we're wheels down."

My seatbelt was snug already. I braced my AR between my knees and gripped the barrel as I watched the carrier grow larger and larger before us. Beekman was bringing us in opposite of the direction which was normal for carrier operations. Planes would impact hard near the stern end of the angled flight deck, and would be stopped by arresting cables by the time they reached the carrier's towering island. We, instead, were approaching from the bow, aiming directly for the narrow sliver of flight deck where planes would be catapulted from during launch.

"Ten seconds," Beekman told us.

The Cessna drifted right and left, the dark grey slab which was our runway pitching slightly from side to side, not a terrible amount of motion from bow to stern. Beekman was correcting, slipping to stay lined up with the deck.

"Crosswind," he said.

He advanced the throttle and steered right, struggling to stay lined up, the carrier seeming to drift away from us.

"Going around!"

Beekman pulled back on the yoke and banked hard left, gaining altitude to line up again for another attempt.

"Fletch..."

I looked back to Schiavo. She nodded to me, signaling to prepare for failure. I reached into the cargo pocket of my pants, ready to retrieve one of the two marine flares I'd stowed there. We'd agreed when finalizing plans for the flight that if we could not land on the carrier, a marine flare, which would generate bright orange smoke as it burned atop the ocean, would signal the *Blue Streak* to turn around. Chris Beekman had been privy to this arrangement, but he was no way in agreement with moving toward that decision.

"Put that away, Fletch," he said, looking to me as the first flare came out of my pocket. "I mean it."

I didn't contest his directive and slipped the flare back where it had come from. Beekman faced forward again and brought the Cessna back into line with the bow of the carrier, beginning another descent toward landing.

"We'll be down in just a minute," Beekman promised.

Down had other meanings than what he intended, I knew. But I also avoided sharing that with our pilot.

Once again, we descended toward the rolling flight deck. And, once again, Beekman maneuvered the Cessna to match the motion of our landing strip. He brought the throttle back as the bow of the carrier pitched upward in a swell, seeming to rise above our position for a moment, making a fiery impact with the steel hull a distinct possibility. But as it had risen, the bow settled again toward the sea, and the deck was positioned just below our flight path.

"Here we go," Beekman said.

There would be no aborted landings this time. As we reached the edge of the flight deck, wheels just a few yards above it, Chris Beekman cut the engines and pushed the yoke forward, doing the opposite of what he would on a normal landing. There was no time here to gently flare the airplane and let its gear set softly down upon the landing surface. He had to get the Cessna down as fast as possible, because only then could he face the next challenge.

Stopping.

The aircraft was jolted by the impact of its three landing gear wheels slamming in unison onto the flight deck. I was thrown forward, almost impaling my face on the barrel of my AR. Two inches to the right and the weapon which I'd planted between my knees, stock down, would have taken out an eye. Not being able to see might have been a blessing right then, though, as when I recovered and looked up I saw the monolithic black cube almost filling the space past the windshield.

Beekman mashed the wheel brakes and the Cessna began to skid, sliding across the wet deck as its nose turned to the left. Completely sideways, I looked out the side window and could see nothing but the towering box racing at me. The tires skated, chattering on the flight deck surface as they sought purchase, finally grabbing hold, the welcome screeching sound of rubber rising. Then, with the right wingtip just feet from the towering obstacle, we stopped.

"Get us tied down!"

Beekman shouted the directive as he shut the Cessna's systems down. I climbed out fast with my AR and did a quick covering sweep of the darkening deck that was visible past the huge block. Schiavo and Martin climbed out behind me, both slinging their weapons and retrieving lengths of pre-cut rope from the baggage compartment in a drill we'd practiced in the hours before taking off.

"Right wing is too close," Schiavo said as the deck rolled gently beneath us, the aircraft shifting a few inches in various directions with each motion of the ship.

"Tie the left side first," Beekman said as he hopped out.

Martin had a rope already cinched to the left main landing gear strut and was feeding it through a tie-down recessed in the deck. Beekman assisted him as Schiavo hustled with the same connection on the right-side strut, pulling her rope taut as the Cessna slid toward her, the just-finished right side tie-downs keeping it from knocking her down. The wingtip was now just inches from the black cube.

"Get it done!" Beekman urged.

I was close enough to assist Schiavo, but my job was simple—covering everyone until the plane was secure. Ahead of me, rising from the right, or starboard, side of the carrier, the island seemed to be the logical place where any threat would materialize. Large steel doors were set into its base, each closed, and above them, on several levels, balconies protruded from the structure. Any one of them could be a sniper's nest where an attacker could pop up at any moment.

None did, though, as the plane was finally tied fully down behind me. Schiavo and Martin grabbed our small backpacks and approached, each armed with an M4. The AK, which had been Martin's preferred long gun for so long, had been traded in in the name of ammunition standardization. The three of us could share magazines if necessary.

Beekman was on his own with his 12 gauge, though. That didn't mean he would be left wanting for ammo. The fifty-round bandolier he retrieved from the baggage compartment and slung across his chest made that quite clear.

"You good with this?" Schiavo asked the pilot.

Beekman walked to where we stood near the corner of the cube and nodded.

"Two rounds from your shotty if something's gone south," she reminded him, the signal pre-arranged.

Whether we would be able to hear it from below the flight deck was an open question.

"Just get back here so we can get off this thing," Beekman said, looking up at the eerily dark and silent island. "I don't have a good feeling about any of this."

Schiavo turned to us as Beekman backed away, taking a position near the tail of the Cessna.

"Let's go," Martin said.

I led off, heading away from the cubic structure now, skirting the edge of the ship closest to the island. There was no way we could know if any of the doors in the superstructure would be unsecured, and no way to know where they led once we were inside if they were. I wasn't even sure if they were technically doors or 'hatches'. None of us knew much of anything about a modern carrier, and those few in Bandon who had some Navy experience, including Clay Genesee, had been able to offer little guidance. Getting lost in some internal maze was not how we needed to start this mission, and so it had been decided before we ever took off that our way to the levels below would be the same as the large cables we could see snaking across the flight deck from the cube.

We'd be taking the forward elevator down.

Not exactly, but we would be utilizing the structure that supported it. The massive lift that had once moved aircraft between the hangar and flight decks was in the down position, allowing the thick bundle of conduit to dive into that space below. We would simply follow those by going over the side, into the open elevator well, sliding down a length of rope.

Simply...

"I'll tie it off," Martin said, slinging his rifle once more as Schiavo and I each took a knee and covered the areas where threats could emerge—the wide flight deck and the dark, open hangar deck below. "Done."

One end of the sturdy rope we'd brought with us was looped solidly through a nearby tie-down. Schiavo tested it with her full body weight, then nodded to me. I had volunteered to be first as we planned our approach to the mission, and now it was time to make good on that. I took the rope and drew the slack up so that I could loop it twice through a carabiner attached to my tactical belt. It was the simplest rappelling method that we could employ that still had a modicum of safety built in. I was no expert at the technique, but I had used it before.

Though I'd never done so on a pitching supercarrier in the middle of the ocean with a darkened space below to greet me.

"See you below," I said and stepped toward the edge of the elevator well.

"Be down in a minute," Schiavo said.

I slung my AR and put my weight on the rope, drawing the slack end behind me as I leaned into the open well. With a slight push off I dropped away, sliding down toward the darkness.

Eight

An expert I was not. The landing I made on the lowered elevator proved that. My boots slipped out from under me and I slid just as the ship rolled to the right. The edge of the elevator before me in the waning light was just that—an edge. *The* edge. Beyond it was the Pacific Ocean.

And I was heading right for it.

I groped at the rope that had slipped from my grip, but it was pulling fast through the carabiner, as fast as I was sliding toward a very wet oblivion. I scrambled for hand and footholds as the end of the rope whipped out of the carabiner and swung away, out of reach.

"Fletch!"

Martin's shout from above meant they could see what had happened. I'd thought my end might have been almost anonymous in the encroaching night, just a splash and a slack rope to indicate I'd gone overboard. My friends witnessing my death didn't make the possibility any more attractive, and I grabbed at the slick surface, jamming a finger into a tie-down and stopping my slide as I heard, and felt, bones in the digit break.

I fought to quell the scream that wanted to come, and used my handhold, and the opposite roll of the ship now beginning, to get myself up and back on track, dashing to some semblance of cover past the inner edge of the elevator.

The hangar deck was as massive as it was dark. Just a hint of ambient dusk filtered in through the elevator wells and smaller openings to the outside. Enough that I was able to bring my weapon up one handed and scan the empty expanse of shifting shadows before me. The injured finger, bent at an unnatural angle, was on my off hand, thankfully. Unfortunately, it was my ring finger, and the swelling that had already begin was pressing painfully all around the wedding band I wore.

"Fletch..."

It was Schiavo. She'd come down as soon as I'd regained my footing. It was immediately apparent to her, with my one-handed hold on my AR, that something was wrong.

"You're hurt," she said.

I showed her my left hand. Even in the din I could see her eyes bug.

"Fletch, you could lose that finger. The circulation is cut off."

"I know," I said, Martin sliding down the rope just behind her.

"What's going on?" he asked as he quickly approached.

He eyed my finger as Schiavo fished a small multitool from her vest, adjusting it so that its jaws were exposed.

"Wire cutters?" I asked, doubtful.

"It's the best we have," she said, looking to Martin. "Cover us."

He moved to a low steel barrier, about waist high, and took a knee, scanning the near blackness that spread out before us.

"We've gotta get that ring off," Schiavo said.

"I know."

She took my hand gently in hers and turned it, placing the cutters in her other hand in position, clamping the tip if the sharpened jaws down on the ring where it arced over the top of my finger.

"Aaahhh," I reacted, as quietly as I could, the cutter head pressing just enough into the damaged flesh to bring on a jolt of pain.

"Not even gonna count," Schiavo said.

And, true to her word, she circled the cutter with both of her hands and bore down, squeezing the jaws together and severing the ring, no *one, two, three* to ease into the action. The pain approached excruciating, but I swallowed the scream I wanted to let out.

"Almost done," Schiavo assured me.

"Just get it off," I urged her.

She gripped the severed ends of the ring with her fingers and spread the soft metal apart until the entire band was a twisted remnant of what it had been.

"Elaine's gonna love the job I did on this," she said, dropping what was left of the ring into one of the cargo pockets in my pants.

It took her another two minutes to quickly, and painfully, straighten and set my fractured finger, wrapping it with thick tape from her small medical kit.

"Nice patch job," I told her through a wave of almost nauseating pain.

"I'm not sure Trey will agree," she said.

"Angela, Fletch..."

We moved to where Martin had found cover, just a few yards away. He was pointing to the cables we'd followed down from above. They snaked across the hangar deck to a point almost precisely halfway across the space. There the twin conduits disappeared through a square hole roughly cut through the thick floor.

"It's going to the reactors," Martin said. "Or generators. Whatever makes power for this beast, that's where these are going."

"Which means that we can just sever these with a charge when the others get here and be done with it," I said, fully aware of the folly of my statement even before I'd given it voice. "Except..."

"Except we don't know what's supposed to come next," Schiavo said. "Whoever did this didn't park a nuclear-powered carrier off our coast just to degrade our radio reception."

"The *Vinson*," Martin said.

Schiavo and I looked to him. He was holding something in one hand. Something small. A thin metal placard of some sort that was partly bent, with rivet holes marking where it had been attached before being pulled from its anchors. "CVN Seventy, the *USS Carl Vinson*. That's where we are."

The ship we'd found, or which had found us, now had a name. My knowledge of naval vessels was limited, but I knew from memory that the *Vinson* was not one of the newest aircraft carriers in the fleet.

"This has been around a while," I said.

"Early eighties," Martin said, then tossed the placard to the floor and half smiled at Schiavo and me. "Micah had every ship catalogued when...when everything started."

Martin's late son had saved Bandon, or Eagle One as it had become known to those seeking refuge, by using his radio and computer skills to redirect a ship carrying supplies from its original destination. That craft, the *Groton Star*, now rested at the bottom of the Pacific after its usefulness had turned into a liability. The boy had done more than secure enough supplies for his town to survive, though. Much more.

"So what do we do?" I asked, my gaze fixed on Schiavo. "Wait for the others or..."

My question trailed off as the sound reached us. Some rhythmic tapping from the far end of the hangar, toward the bow of the ship.

"We're all hearing that, right?" Martin asked, quietly now.

Schiavo and I both nodded, each of us bringing our rifles up slightly, the action seeming a somewhat odd response to exactly what we were hearing.

"That's a horse, right?" Martin pressed.

"That's what I'm hearing," I said.

A horse. Trotting or galloping, or whatever it was that horses did, though they *did not* do so on an aircraft carrier, to the best of my knowledge.

"Orville's going to be here any minute," Martin said.

The *Blue Streak* was scheduled to arrive soon, as my friend had said. And with it Sergeants Westin and Hart, along with Corporal Laws. Our priority had to be getting them aboard safely.

Almost equal with that as an imperative was ensuring we weren't all heading into some ambush, though the almost impossible sound of a horse did not point toward that. It did, however, indicate life aboard. A presence. And that, we knew, could spell danger in many ways.

"Martin, you stay here," Schiavo instructed her husband. "Fletch and I will scout toward the stern. If the *Blue Streak* shows up, call out."

Martin could have resisted her, but didn't. This was her role. Leader. Making decisions was part and parcel of that. Heeding her wishes, despite their relationship, was his responsibility.

"Don't go exploring," Martin said.

"Just there and back," Schiavo assured him.

We moved aft, slowly, cautiously, the carrier shifting beneath us. Despite being anchored, the unchecked motion of the Pacific moved the massive ship like ripples in a bathtub played with a rubber duck. The ocean ruled out here. All things manmade were at its mercy.

The darkness deepened and ebbed as we moved further aft. The day's waning light drizzled in through the aft elevator openings on both port and starboard sides, enough to reveal something ahead.

Something.
"Fletch..."
"I see it," I said.

Nine

Resolving out of the darkness, maybe fifty feet in front of us, was a wall of fabric suspended from the ceiling of the hangar deck, its bottom edge secured to tie-downs on the floor. It shifted easily in the breeze that whooshed through the hangar deck, billowing the black cloth against its anchors, moving enough that, as we neared it, we could see that it was not a single bolt of material, but several positioned next to each other. We moved toward one of those separations, the obvious clomping of hooves growing louder as we did. Louder, but also...stranger.

"Does that sound off to you?" I asked Schiavo quietly.

She nodded and paused near one of the natural slits in the barrier.

"It's not real," she said.

I reached to the fabric and peeled one edge aside, aiming my AR through and activating the weapon light fixed to the side of the handguard, the beam cutting through the darkness to reveal a metal stool maybe thirty feet away. Atop it rested a small digital music player, cable connecting it to a portable speaker at the base of the stool, the sound that had drawn us amplified through it.

Schiavo took the other edge of the fabric in hand and ripped it aside, stepping through with her own weapon light switched on. I followed her into the space, a rough circle created by the lengths of dark cloth, our rifles sweeping the area.

"No one," I said.

"Not now," she said, moving toward the stool and stopping the sound from the player. "But someone was here to turn that on."

If that was true, then we were being watched.

"Kill your light, Fletch."

We both did at the same time, then headed for the tear in the fabric Schiavo had made. Just yards from it we both stopped dead in our tracks.

Footsteps...

Schiavo and I looked to each other in the near darkness. Someone was coming. More than one. More than two, I thought, though beyond that it was impossible to tell. But there was a definite presence approaching. Individuals moving toward us. Carefully. Stalking.

We were being hunted.

Schiavo nudged my shoulder and motioned to her left. We moved that way until we were almost at the edge of the fabric barrier closest to the port side of the ship. She took a prone position, and I followed her lead, placing myself five yards from her, both of us aiming at where we'd passed through the cloth wall.

Where's Martin?

That obvious question rose suddenly in my thoughts, and I was certain that Schiavo had wondered the same thing. Whoever was coming our way would have had to move within sight of him, maybe even right past him depending on where they'd entered the hangar deck. Or they could have just been waiting in the shadows while we rappelled down.

There was an even more pressing question, though— were they friend or foe? Despite the signal that had blinded our communications, this was a Navy vessel. That there would be sailors or Marines aboard was not beyond the realm of what was possible, no matter how odd the circumstances. We could have announced ourselves, and

who we were, but until we knew for certain we were facing
friendlies, that would have to wait.

Our wait was exactly two seconds.

Those advancing on us opened fire simultaneously,
rounds shredding the fabric and tearing into the stool
beyond, music player and speaker blasted into bits of tiny
electronic shrapnel. We'd shifted our position and were
clear of being hit. But that wouldn't last.

"Take them," Schiavo said.

She fired first, and I followed a second later. I'd
removed the suppressor from my AR before we'd departed,
a decision based upon weight and perceived necessity. It
lengthened the weapon, and, if we'd needed to move
through narrow passageways I thought it would become a
hindrance. As it was, with both Schiavo and I firing, and the
unseen attackers some twenty yards from us, the noise was
utterly deafening.

Screams...

I heard them. One, two, then three as our return fire
found its mark. The incoming rounds shifted toward our
positions now, muzzle flashes muted beyond the wall of
cloth. Each, to us, became targets, Schiavo and I squeezing
off bursts toward every pulse of brightness, hearing more
cries mixed among the automatic fire, and the clank of
weapons falling to the floor, and then it was over.

The gunfire ended, but there was no silence. Moaning,
from two distinct voices, crossed the distance between us
and our attackers. We had no idea if we'd hit them all, or if
some had fled. But the agonized sounds that remained told
us that some possibility of a threat still existed.

"Dead men don't pull triggers," I said quietly to
Schiavo.

She nodded and rose from her prone position, staying
low. I followed her lead. We each backed away, until we
were at the far end of the fabric barrier. As I continued to

provide cover, Schiavo used a knife to cut an opening in the cloth. She stepped through. A second later I did the same.

The hangar deck was darker, the last light of day that had drifted through the elevator wells faded now to almost nothing. Yet we didn't dare turn our lights on again as we advanced along the perimeter of the billowing wall, moving forward, Schiavo exposed to my left. Without warning she stopped, her M4 zeroed in on something.

I slipped left, past her, covering the shadowy space before us. Even in the din I could see why she'd stopped.

Bodies.

They were almost piled atop each other, six, their weapons scattered. We'd heard the sounds of two attackers moaning, but only one moved, his helmeted head tipping back and forth, eyes barely open.

"Cover me," Schiavo said quietly.

I did as she stepped close to the fallen attackers, verifying that five were dead, and one not far from paying that ultimate price.

"Fletch..."

I shifted closer, alternating my attention between Schiavo and the rolling darkness that surrounded us.

"Who are you?" Schiavo asked the survivor, leaning close. "Why did you come at us?"

The man gave no answer. I wasn't even sure he could hear the question he'd been asked. And neither mattered a few seconds later as a last, long breath slipped past his lips and his head settled to one side.

Schiavo brought her M4 up again but stayed on one knee.

"Look at them," she said, her voice still hushed against any who might still be lurking in the blackness. "That's all new gear."

Special Ops helmets, which bore a passing resemblance to something a cyclist or a hockey player might wear. Short-barreled M4s with double mags clamped together and pristine ACOG sights.

"It's Tacti-cool, Fletch," she said. "They had the gear but not the skillset."

"These guys weren't military," I said. "They were playing the part."

"Why?" Schiavo asked, standing now. "And for who?"

There was no apparent answer to that. Not even after we performed a cursory search of the bodies, finding not a thing of importance. No personal possessions. No rings or watches. Nothing but what they wore and what they'd carried into their losing battle.

"All right," Schiavo said.

She turned her attention toward the bow. To the place we'd come from.

"Let's get back to Martin."

Those were her words, but there was more she did not say, but which I knew she was thinking. Fears as to why he hadn't intervened, or responded once the firefight began. Those things she held to herself as we made our way along the pitchy and pitching hangar deck toward where her husband, and my friend, should be.

Ten

He was gone.

"Martin," I said, not shouting, but not hushed, either.

Schiavo moved quickly past me as we reached the spot near the starboard forward elevator where he'd positioned himself. Her weapon was still up, scanning the emptiness where her husband had been. Where he was supposed to be.

"Martin," she called to him, making no attempt to quiet herself.

I looked over the floor nearby, searching for any sign of what might have happened. Dropped equipment signaling a struggle. Blood indicating a wound. But there was nothing.

Martin Jay was simply gone.

"Where is he, Fletch?"

I couldn't answer that. As it was, there was no time to even discuss the issue as, when I glanced behind toward the elevator, I could very plainly see a boat approaching on the choppy water, its shape silhouetted by the last wisps of daylight trickling eastward from the horizon.

The *Blue Streak* had arrived.

"The boat," I said.

Schiavo looked and saw it, too. A dozen things were racing through her thoughts right then, I knew. Martin. Getting her men aboard. Completing our mission. There was a hierarchy to what needed to happen, and in what order. It was no more complicated than 'first things first'.

"Deploy the rope and signal the boat," Schiavo told me. "I'll cover."

She dropped to a knee behind the same low barrier which Martin had placed himself. I focused on my part, retrieving a seventy-five foot length of knotted rope from my small backpack and moving out onto the lowered elevator. One end of the rope I secured to a tie-down, and the other I heaved over the edge, the coiled end landing with a barely audible splash atop the churning sea. Next I took out my flashlight and signaled with three quick pulses. Without delay the same response came from the boat and it maneuvered close to the carrier, disappearing from view as it slid beneath the elevator. I inched out toward the edge, holding the rope until I felt it go taut. The first climber was on it.

"They're coming aboard," I reported to Schiavo, glancing quickly behind to see the dim shape of her giving me a quick thumbs-up.

Thirty seconds later a gloved hand reached over the edge of the elevator. I took hold of the rope and reached out, grabbing the arm of the first to make it aboard.

It was Hart, the medic, his medical pack thick on his back. I helped him over the edge and hauled him clear of the rope, which went taut again, the next member of the team making their way aboard.

"We could have hauled your pack up on a second line," I told Hart as he got to his feet.

He shook his head and nodded to the active ocean.

"I figured we might not have time to throw a rope to haul gear," Hart said. "Orville said he's having trouble staying close, and it's too deep for him to anchor here."

The sheer bulk of the ship, which muted the worst of the pummeling waves, still allowed an uncomfortable roll to be transmitted aboard. What that was like on the much smaller *Blue Streak* I couldn't imagine right then.

"What's the depth?" I asked.

"He said there's a plateau here," the medic answered. "Maybe four hundred feet. He said it slopes down to seven thousand feet between here and Bandon."

I recalled some bit of trivial detail from a documentary I'd seen long ago. It had been about ships and their anchors. One fact the program shared was that aircraft carrier anchor chains could be a thousand feet long. To me that meant that those who'd brought the ship here had to choose this exact point to anchor it. Any closer in the shallows nearer to Bandon would have made the *Vinson* more accessible to us, and more vulnerable to any action we might take.

"Any signs of life?" Hart asked.

"Yeah," I answered. "Not friendlies."

He brought his M4 up to a ready position and moved off to join his commander just inside the hangar deck. Corporal Laws came up next, followed by Sergeant Westin.

"Orville's gonna pull back and stand off from the carrier," he told me. "We almost bashed into the hull down there."

"Okay," I said.

The fishing boat emerged from its place beneath the elevator and rode the waves to a position a hundred yards off the starboard bow. I flashed him three times, and he acknowledged with the same, then Westin, Laws, and I joined Schiavo and Hart in the nearly full darkness of the hangar deck.

"Martin is missing," Hart told his comrades, Schiavo having briefed him.

She explained what we'd found, and who, to the new arrivals.

"No sign at all?" Westin checked.

"None," I said.

"Ma'am," Hart said, drawing his leader's attention. "What are your orders?"

The mission's objective had not changed, though some parameters had. We were facing some sort of enemy, one seemingly inept at first blush. But we were also confronted by loss. One of our number was missing. Schiavo had to, at least momentarily, put these shifting situational sands aside and focus on what had to be done.

I didn't know if I could do what she had to.

"Sgt. Westin..."

"Yes, ma'am."

Schiavo motioned to the cables stretching from the elevator well to the hole cut in the hangar deck floor.

"Consensus is that those are feeding power to whatever is in the structure on deck," she said. "You have the charges?"

"I do," Westin confirmed. "I think a pound should cut those clean. There'll be a shockwave in this confined space."

"We'll take cover," Schiavo said. "Get it done."

Westin nodded and headed to the cable nearest to where it disappeared through the hole.

"I'll cover him, ma'am," Corporal Laws said, then followed his comrade.

"Over there," I said, gesturing to a protected space behind a short structural rib protruding from the side wall of the hangar deck. "We should be good there."

"Good," Schiavo said, scanning the darkness, for threats, and for some answer to where her husband could possibly be.

Less than a minute after heading to place the charges, Westin and Laws hurried back.

"One-minute fuse," Westin said.

Schiavo pointed to the area of cover we'd found. We all moved that way, maintaining cover across the open expanse before us. Just beyond the thick slab of steel we huddled against the hangar deck wall, waiting. For the explosion. For some attack that might materialize out of the darkness as one had before.

The latter didn't come. The former did, in the form of a blinding flash and a sharp crack that reverberated in the space, echoing with painful force over and over, the metal structure seeming to vibrate like some tuning fork for nearly half a minute. When the noise subsided, there was only that same darkness and a veil of misty smoke blowing in the shifting air.

"Corporal Laws, have a look."

The young man, who'd become that on our journey through the hellfire to Portland, and beyond, didn't hesitate. As we moved back to our original position nearer the elevator to cover him, he jogged smoothly into the hazy darkness to assess how the charge had worked.

"Fletch..."

Schiavo was next to me, speaking softly as we waited for Laws' return.

"Yeah?"

"I'm kind of at a loss here," she said, hinting at a vulnerability which was natural, but not for her.

"We'll find him," I assured her.

She stared off into the interior night that stretched across the hangar deck. I'd expected a nod of acknowledgment, if not agreement. But I received none. She was truly, deeply thrown by the disappearance of her husband.

Eleven

"He's coming," Hart said.

Schiavo looked fast, her reaction instinctual. But it was not Martin who had returned. It was Carter Laws running toward us, the lingering smoke swirling in the wake he cut through it.

"It's sliced clean through," he reported.

"Sergeant, do a radio check," Schiavo said, forcing herself to stay on task.

This choreography, too, had been pre-arranged. Westin retrieved a handheld transmitter from his gear and stepped onto the elevator, looking out to where the *Blue Streak* would be, holding station several hundred meters away. He turned the unit on and adjusted the squelch and volume, looking back to us with a relieved smile.

"No jamming," he said.

"Try it out," Schiavo said.

Westin brought the handheld unit to his face and keyed the mic.

"*Blue Streak*, do you copy?"

There wasn't even a delay for dramatic effect.

"Well that is a welcome sound," Orville Pehrsson replied over the airwaves. "We're back in business."

Schiavo stepped out from cover and motioned for her come expert to hand her the radio. He did and turned to face the interior of the hangar deck, covering his commander.

"Orville, this is Colonel Schiavo. Will you be able to approach the carrier again to recover personnel?"

Now there was a brief pause, though the drama was not for effect. It was rooted in an unpleasant reality.

"I don't believe so, Angela," Orville replied.

Schiavo kept the radio close to her cheek and thought for a moment, weighing risks and alternatives. The answer she came up with surprised us all.

"Orville, take the *Blue Streak* back to Bandon," Schiavo instructed the fisherman over the radio. "Your boat getting smashed to pieces out here will serve no purpose."

"But how will you..."

He didn't finish the question, likely because he knew she would.

"We have other transport," she reminded him. "Just get yourself safely home. Copy?"

"Aye," Orville said. "I copy."

The transmission ended and she handed the radio back to Westin, eyeing it for a moment as he slipped it into his pack.

"Any chance you can reach Bandon on that?"

Westin shook his head at his commander's question.

"Not enough power, and too short an antenna," he said.

"There are still some antennas on the island," she said.

The superstructure rising from the starboard side of the flight deck appeared to have had much of its upper communication array stripped away. But not all of it.

"Could you use what's up there?" Schiavo pressed. "Tap into one of those antennas and use it to transmit?"

"Possibly," Westin said. "I'd still need more power."

"This ship has power," Schiavo said. "We know that. There could be some still flowing to the island."

Westin nodded, accepting that.

"Then, yes, ma'am. I can make it happen."

"What are you thinking, Angela?" I asked.

"There's no way Orville can get any of us off," she said. "With him gone, the only point of contact between us and Bandon is that aircraft up top. We may not have time to play carrier pigeon passing messages if I we have to contact Bandon."

"We need a radio," I said.

"We need a radio," she affirmed.

"Ma'am," Laws said.

"Corporal..."

"The plane...it only holds three passengers."

"And there are six of us," Schiavo said.

She ignored Martin's absence. She had to. We all did. He *would* be back with us before we departed the *Vinson*.

"Yes, ma'am."

"Two flights," Schiavo said. "Mr. Beekman is going to have to play taxi driver a bit more than planned."

"We'll leave in shifts," Hart said.

"Once we've figured this out, and once we're all here, that's how we'll get home."

No one challenged her plan for the ultimate evacuation of the carrier. Except me.

"And what if not everyone we find aboard wants to kill us?"

She might have considered the possibility and dismissed it, but I didn't think so.

"If that happens, Fletch, we'll deal with it," she answered, a subtle sharpness in her tone. "But right now that's way down on the list of things I'm worried about."

It wasn't a rebuke that came from animus, but the others noticed her harsh reply. Even Angela recognized the biting reply she'd offered, and for an instant she quieted, berating herself internally, I suspected.

But she had to move on. *We* had to move on. And she was the one who had to get us moving.

"Sgt. Hart, you'll stay with Fletch and me," Schiavo ordered. "Sgt. Westin, you and Corporal Laws will get to the flight deck and see what you can do about getting us a working radio while you help Mr. Beekman keep that plane secure."

Westin nodded and looked to the rope we'd used to rappel down to the hangar deck.

"Can you make it up on that?" she asked.

"Not a problem," Westin said, and slung his M4. "Corporal..."

Laws did the same, the pair moving quickly to the rope and expertly making their way toward the flight deck.

"That leaves us," Schiavo said once they were safely topside.

"Ma'am, what you already found," Hart began, "it sounds...odd."

Sounds of a galloping horse being played through speakers and an attack by men who were more caricature of soldiers than the real thing...yes, I thought, odd started to describe what we'd seen and heard already.

"And what does that mean, Sergeant?" Schiavo asked.

Hart didn't hesitate. She'd trained him well.

"Expect the unexpected," the medic said.

"Okay," I said, my weapon ready as I looked to the darkness that Hart had been covering. "Let's go find Martin."

He was Schiavo's husband. He was the man who'd saved Bandon. And he was my friend. As much as she wanted to be reunited with him, I knew that there was no way that I was going to leave the carrier without him by my side.

"Lead off, Fletch," Schiavo said.

I did just that, leaving the meager cover we'd used, and walking slowly into the darkness.

Twelve

I hadn't taken twenty steps toward the bow when I came upon something.

Something that could have killed me.

"Hold up," I said quietly, putting a hand out to signal the others to stay back.

"What is it?" Schiavo asked.

I crouched and cautiously approached what I'd spotted just a couple yards before it might have swallowed me—a square hole cut into the floor of the hangar deck. It was roughly the shape and size of the penetration which the huge power cables had passed through to the lower decks, its edges jagged, knots of once molten steel protruding from where some welding torch had pushed aggressively through the thick metal. Past its edge there was only darkness below. I'd only seen the shadowy breach because I'd been looking. What if Martin hadn't been? What if he'd been maneuvering for an advantage when the assault began, or to cut off any reinforcements? Would he have seen the hole in time to avoid it?

I waved Schiavo and Hart forward. The medic positioned himself off to the left of us, providing cover.

"What is it?" Schiavo asked.

I pointed to the hole.

"A first attempt to pass the cables up from below?" I suggested.

Schiavo nodded. Even in the night now fully filling the hangar deck, I could see the fear build in her gaze. She was thinking exactly what I had about Martin, and what might have happened.

"Light it up, Fletch."

I shifted my position first, slightly away from Schiavo, wanting that separation should my weapon light trigger some violent response from below. She brought her M4 up and took aim down into the hole, ready to respond.

"Now," I said.

The beam sliced the darkness past the barrel of my AR and lit up the space below, immediately revealing that Martin was not there. But some sign of him was.

"Fletch..."

"I see it," I told Schiavo.

The space below, some sort of compartment, had been cleared out, just the slab that had once been the missing piece of deck before us lying on the floor some fifteen feet below. And on it was scrawled something. Scratched with the point of a sharp object. A message.

MJ...

And next to those very clear initials for Martin Jay was a single arrow, pointing to an opening in the compartment, a narrow passageway partly visible beyond.

"He fell," Schiavo said. "It could have killed him."

Fifteen feet was substantial. But depending on how he landed, he could have been lucky enough to walk away with only bruises. That he wasn't there, and had left some message, pointed strongly to him not being severely injured.

"Why isn't he still there?" she wondered.

"Maybe it was either leave or be captured," I said.

"That message would help any pursuers as much as it does us," she said. "Maybe more. They have to know the layout of this ship."

"The best worst option might have been all he had," I told her.

To see any further, to learn more, we would have to venture below.

And I knew we would.

"Sgt. Hart..."

The medic shifted closer to our position and glanced at what we'd found.

"Secure a rope," Schiavo said. "We're going down. All of us."

* * *

The rope Hart tied off to a structural beam made the descent far less treacherous than it must have been for Martin. I went down first and covered the doorway to the passage outside the compartment as Schiavo and Hart followed. There was no option to advance without using artificial light down here, but we didn't have to be excessive about it.

"One light on at a time," Schiavo ordered.

Doing so would clearly expose whichever of us was employing the light, but the others might be able to reach cover if a firefight erupted. It seemed we were facing our own best worst option.

"What is this room?" Hart asked, scanning the space we'd come into.

Whatever it was it had been stripped bare, metal attachment points on the walls ripped away, either by brute force or at the business end of a welder's torch.

"I think this was meant for the cables," I said. "They cleared it out to fit them through. But it didn't work out, for some reason."

"Meaning they make mistakes," Hart said.

That was a fairly large mistake to make, considering the effort they'd undertaken to power some hellish transmitter affixed to the flight deck. It spoke of amateurish planning, which matched the level of professionalism they'd exhibited in their attack.

"And still they have an aircraft carrier," I said, voicing the ultimate juxtaposition.

"Fletch, are you okay staying on point?"

"I am," I told Schiavo.

The passageway just outside the compartment ran left and right, a bare steel wall just across from the doorway. I killed my weapon light and leaned quickly through the doorway, looking and aiming left, activating the light for just a second. The corridor stretched out before me, doors set into either side at varying intervals, piping and conduit affixed to the metal ceiling above. Nothing of note stood out, and I repeated the action with the same haste looking to the right, finding a similar layout. The first recon complete, I leaned back into the compartment.

"Both ways end in T intersections," I reported.

The light of my downcast weapon light bounced off the floor and lit Schiavo from below, raising deep, angular shadows from her features as she considered our next move.

"We could split up," Hart suggested as he covered the opening above us.

"No," Schiavo said. "I'm not losing anyone else because they were alone."

In that statement I knew that she blamed herself for Martin's disappearance, at least in part. It was an honest, if inaccurate appraisal of responsibility common to leaders who had lost people.

But we hadn't lost Martin. We simply hadn't found him. Yet.

"Right is toward the bow," Schiavo said, sizing up the maritime landscape we were facing. "There's not much bow left."

"There can't be much that way," I said.

"Left then?" Hart asked.

"Let's move toward the stern," Schiavo said. "If we don't find him, we'll check the bow on our way back."

Noah Mann

The implication was that we'd be leaving the way we came, through the hole above us. But there were obviously other ways to reach the hangar deck. Those who'd attacked us had emerged from some door or passage unseen in the darkness. In the maze of corridors and stairs and ladders and compartments we were certain to come across, there was no guarantee that we would be able to locate an alternate way out. Finding our way back to this point of egress was going to be a big enough challenge.

"Someone should keep track of our route," I suggested.

"I'll map us," Hart said. "Up here."

He tapped his temple.

"Years of role playing games has prepared me for just this moment," the medic shared with a smile. "It's just a big dungeon in my head."

Schiavo, too, allowed a brief grin. It lasted just a few seconds.

"Let's get moving, Fletch."

I did as Schiavo said and stepped through the doorway, bringing my AR up and activating the light as I turned left. The corridor lit up before me and we were on our way into the depths of the carrier.

Thirteen

There was no rhyme or reason to the path we took, particularly with no further clues left by Martin. No trail of bread crumbs to follow. We moved along the passageways, turning left, right, checking compartments. And finding nothing. Not a single sign of any life.

Then we heard the sound.

It rose from a steep stairwell as we were about to pass it. A tapping. Metal on metal. Not rhythmic. No cadence or meaning to it. But still, it was there.

Schiavo activated her weapon light and aimed it down the stairs, hardly more than a wide ladder angled steeply between the decks. I maintained my watch ahead, covering the way we'd been moving, chancing a glance down the stairwell.

As I did the sound stopped.

"A sound stopping is as telling as a sound starting," Schiavo said.

As if to prove her right, a few seconds later, the sound rose again, the *tap-taptap-tap-tapping* a clear indication of...

Something.

"Fletch..."

I backed up and put my light down the stairwell, gripping my AR one handed as I took hold of the handrail and made my way down the steep steps.

* * *

"Straight ahead," I told Schiavo when she and Hart were behind me.

"Okay," she said.

We were two levels below the hangar deck now. Was that even the proper term? Level? No, they were decks, too. But clearing that up in my thought process wasn't getting us any closer to locating the source of the sound.

I moved forward, the beam of my light splashing off the grey metal walls, the space eerily reminiscent of the ashen world left behind by the blight. We passed intersecting corridors and more compartments, giving each a cursory check as we progressed toward the sound, which appeared to be emanating from beyond a slightly open door at the end of the passageway a dozen yards distant.

"Low on your right," Schiavo told me softly.

The drill was almost ingrained. I would open the door and use my light while sweeping the space at eye level. Schiavo would crouch on my right. Hart would bring up the rear, offering cover for any threats behind and to back us up should that become necessary.

I reached the door, another corridor stretching left and right from it. A quick check showed both directions clear. My focus shifted fully to what had to be done.

Tap-taptap-tap-tap...

The sound continued. Standing this close to it now, just a hinged slab of steel separating it from us, there was no doubt remaining that it was not random at all. There was purpose to it.

Just as that fact became clear, we heard the whistling. It, like the tapping, came from whatever lay beyond the barely open door, each matching the other's tempo. A man's whistle, it seemed, not halting, but strained.

Schiavo lowered herself into position and nodded. I pushed the door, the heavy barrier swinging slowly, creaking on dry hinges. My light swept left, revealing another stripped compartment.

Stripped, but not empty.

A chair rested against the back wall, maybe ten feet away, and in the chair a naked man sat smiling at us, one hand clenched to his stomach, the other hanging at his side, gripping a long knife, blood dripping from it.

"She was right," the man said upon seeing us. "She really was right."

I stepped into the space and swept the room with my light, the man its only occupant. The knife blade tapped the leg of the chair a few more times then slipped from his fingers, blood continuing to flow from a pair of long gashes across his wrist.

"Who are you?" I asked, Schiavo and Hart following me in.

The man didn't reply. He simply beamed at us, his gaze swimming as if some marvelous truth had been confirmed.

"You're hurt," Schiavo said. "We can help you."

He lifted his hand and gazed at the deep cuts, red bubbles pulsing with each beat of his heart.

"It wasn't enough," the man said.

"I have a medic with me," Schiavo said.

The man looked to us, the glare of my weapon light sparkling off his eyes as I maintained a cautious aim on his chest. He shook his head, still smiling.

"That won't be necessary," he said, then eased the clenched hand away from his chest, revealing a grenade in his grip.

"No pin!" Hart warned.

The pin which should have been in place to make the weapon safe was gone, presumably pulled by the man. Schiavo pushed her medic backward, away from the threat. Hart spun, catching a foot on the metal frame of the door. He tumbled to the floor, blocking the way out.

"Goodbye," the man said, easing his hold on the grenade, the safety lever releasing.

A soft pop signaled that the internal fuse had been lit.

"Go!" I shouted.

Hart got to one knee and reached for his commander, pulling her through the doorway as I moved to exit. Too fast, it turned out.

Where Hart had tripped himself up on the hardened door jamb, my boot caught on Schiavo's as she was hustled clear. I fell sideways, beyond the door.

One second...

Two seconds...

That's how long it had been from the instant the man ignited the fuse. He didn't hurl the grenade in our direction, instead cupping it gently, serenely against his chest. How long was the fuse on the type of weapon he held? Three seconds? Four?

I couldn't know for sure, and there was no time to chance the effort it would take to make it out of the room. As I heard Schiavo and Hart tumble into the corridor outside, in the clear, I pushed myself up and against the door that had swung almost fully inward, putting it between me and the suicidal man.

At the instant I made it to my feet the grenade detonated.

There was sound, and smoke, and a pulse of fire to accompany the wild spray of shrapnel that ricocheted about in the confines of the steel compartment, but the greatest effect I felt was the heavy steel door, which had shielded me from the worst of the blast, slamming into me as the concussive wave hit it. I was smashed against the wall behind, almost crushed between it and the door, the impact stunning me. The world went dark for a moment, smoke choking me and voices screaming my name through the echoing ring that filled my head.

"Fletch!"

I lay crumpled on the floor as Schiavo and Hart pulled the door away, sound and light seeming twisted. The haze that surrounded me, that surrounded them, gave everything I saw an almost angelic blur. If the stench of burning flesh hadn't been so pervasive I might have thought I was seeing actual angels.

"Fletch!"

"Yeah," I said, then coughed for a full ten seconds as Hart helped his commander lift me from the floor.

"Get him out of here," Schiavo said.

As they pulled me around the door, the swinging light on the AR slung across my front passed over the man. Or what was left of him. A large red stain covered the wall behind where he'd sat, and the mangled chair that had supported him, along with his body below the hips, lay in a heap in the corner, tossed there by the violent explosion. That was all there was.

"We need a safe space," Schiavo said as they helped me from the horrific scene. "Down that way."

They half carried, half dragged me down the hall to the left, Schiavo clearing the way with her M4's light, searching for a suitable room to regroup.

"Here," she said.

She and Hart pulled me into a compartment that was not as bare as the others we'd come across previously. Two chairs were toppled in the space. Hart righted one and Schiavo eased me into it, stripping my weapons and gear until I sat there, wobbly, just my clothing and boots left. Hart closed the door. It was not a watertight barrier, and there was no lock on it, just a knob that turned freely.

"Sergeant check him out," Schiavo said.

Hart dropped his gear as his commander covered the door. He knelt next to me, supporting me with one hand while examining me.

"Can you hear me, Fletch?"

"Yeah, Trey," I said. "You and the church bells ringing in my head."

"That should pass," he assured me.

He ran his hands over me from head to toe, shaking his head when he was done.

"Not a scratch," Hart said, amazed. "Be thankful you weren't behind this door."

He tipped his head toward the barrier Schiavo was covering. It was some sort of synthetic material made to look like wood. The space we'd taken refuge in, it seemed, had been some sort of office aboard the carrier in its more useful days.

"Navy steel saved your life, Fletch," Hart said.

"Is he all right to continue?" Schiavo asked.

"Yeah," Hart said, repacking his medical gear. "Doesn't even need a bandage. Just a few minutes to get his wits back."

"Okay," Schiavo said, glancing back to me. "And your opinion?"

"I'm okay," I said. "But I don't want to do that again."

Hart let me sit for a few minutes then helped me back into my gear when I insisted on standing.

"Who do you think that guy was?" Hart asked.

"I'm more interested in who the 'she' was he kept mentioning," I said.

There were enough oddities thus far to occupy our discussion for hours. But we didn't have hours, because Martin might not.

"We know one thing from that whole fiasco," Schiavo said. "Martin didn't come this way."

"He wouldn't have missed grenade guy," I agreed. "So do we backtrack or press another direction?"

"Let's head down one of these corridors and see if it will circle back to those stairs," Schiavo said.

I picked my AR up from where Hart had leaned it against the wall and snapped it onto the sling across my gear vest.

"I'm ready," I said.

"Hart is point," Schiavo said.

I understood her shifting me off the lead of our short column. I felt back in the game, but was I really? The effects of the blast had largely worn off, but would any resurface? She needed a fresh set of eyes, and ears, clearing the way for us.

"I'll tailgun," I said.

"Get us moving, Sergeant."

"Yes, ma'am."

* * *

We did as Schiavo had said, Hart leading us left out of the room we'd hunkered down it, then right, searching for a connecting corridor which would take us back toward the bow of the ship.

Instead, we came upon another anomaly to add to the horse sounds and the naked man with the grenade.

"This makes no sense," Hart said, stopping us.

Just beyond him, where the way forward should be, a slab of steel had been crudely welded, blocking the passage. Its edges were uneven, and several gaps existed on its perimeter, the largest just big enough to shine a light through.

"Let me look, sergeant," Schiavo said.

She stepped to the barrier and took a small flashlight from her vest, shining it through the opening as she eased her face close to the opening for a look, recoiling quickly before seeing anything, a sour look upon her face.

"What is it?" I asked.

Schiavo stepped aside and let me have a look for myself. But it wasn't anything within sight that elicited her reaction, nor mine as I put my face to the opening.

It was what I smelled.

"Oh man," I saw, backing away.

"Fletch?" Hart asked.

"Decomp," I said.

Fourteen

The sickly-sweet stench that drizzled through the opening meant that death lay somewhere beyond the barrier. Recent death. Not the kind that had been commonplace in the months and years after the blight. There would be no remains nearly mummified by stale air sitting in some living room rocker. That was a lengthy process witnessed by many who set out on scouting and scavenging missions from our earliest days in Bandon.

No, what we would find, if we made it past the blockage, were those who'd gone to meet their maker within days of our arrival on the *Vinson*.

"That's from more than just one body," Schiavo said.

Not far from where we stood were the decomposing remains of human beings. Whether we would ever know who they were, or why and how they died, was an open question.

"We're not getting past that," I said.

"Unless we blow it," Hart said. "I have two charges. Ed wanted me to bring some backups in case anything happened to his."

Sergeant Ed Westin had blown the power cables to the transmitter on deck, and was, at that moment, attempting to rig some sort of communications system to reach beyond the carrier. Because of Hart we had the means to breach the barrier, but should we?

"Let's find another way to—"

The sudden rush of light cut Schiavo off. Up and down the corridors, and in compartments off of the passageways, lights flickered to life all at once, cold fluorescents clicking then humming as they warmed up. Even beyond the makeshift wall we'd encountered the lights had come on, a shaft of brightness angling through the small opening at its edge.

Schiavo killed her flashlight beam and pocketed it.

"Someone has control somewhere," Schiavo said.

"Over there," I told her, motioning to the barrier. "You barricade the center. You protect what deserves protecting."

She nodded, unconcerned.

"There's no point in breaking through," Schiavo said. "Martin didn't. He has to be on this side."

"Unless there's another way through," Hart said.

She shook her head.

"We stick with the plan," she said. "Find him, and then we figure out the rest."

We turned away from the barrier, Hart still in the lead. The ringing in my ears had almost totally subsided, and the feeling that I'd been punched in the gut by some behemoth boxer was fading as well. I wasn't a hundred percent yet after almost being blown up.

Three times...

This was the third time I'd been faced with death by explosives. From a nuke while we hunkered down in a missile control center beneath the Wyoming wastelands. In the pit in Skagway as the Russian forces were taken out. And now at sea, by a crazy man with a grenade.

She was right...

His words bubbled up in my thoughts and nagged at me as we turned left, then right, and followed a long passageway. Schiavo couldn't afford to consider what the man had told us, but I couldn't avoid doing that very thing.

She really was right...

Someone, a woman, had meant something to the naked man. A woman who had told him something that came to pass. But what had come to pass?

Our presence.

It had seemed to be the catalyst for the man's reaction, and for his decision to finish himself off after an unsuccessful attempt at suicide in the hours before we came upon him. If our arrival, our showing ourselves to him, was the thing the unknown woman had been right about, then there was some importance placed upon it.

And upon us.

But why?

It was the parallel question to go with our wondering as to why the carrier had anchored itself in the proximity of Bandon. My concern that we were, yet again, a target, seemed to be given credence by what the man's crazed words implied.

Someone, some woman, had expected us to do exactly what we had done—come to the carrier.

"Angela," I said.

Schiavo glanced behind as we kept moving.

"What happened on the hangar deck was a trap," I said.

"I know that, Fletch."

"I don't think we're done with that sort of thing."

"Because we were expected," she said.

Contrary to what I'd thought, Schiavo had been entertaining the same line of reasoning which had just struck me. Even in the midst of the chaos, with the man she loved missing, she was pressing on and weighing all angles which might explain, in some small way, just what the purpose of all this was.

Fifteen

We cleared the deck, and the one we'd come down from, finding more welded barriers which seemed to cut the center section of the carrier's lower decks off from the rest of the ship. Heading even deeper, several decks further down, the same blockades, at roughly the same points, appeared to confirm that belief.

And nowhere did we find Martin, nor any sign of him.

"Almost everything has been stripped," Hart commented as we paused to regroup on the lowest deck we'd been able to reach. "It's like they cleaned up before they did all this reconfiguring."

He nodded toward the final barrier we'd found, in a central passageway cramped by thick pipes and conduits. It was the last way possible to access the center portion of the ship, and it was blocked like all the other avenues to continue had been.

"He's not here, Angela," I said.

Schiavo stared at the blockage and nodded, knowing what that meant.

"If he's not on this side of the barriers..."

"Then he found a way to the other side," I completed the suggestion for her.

"Why would he do that?" Hart asked. "If he fell and was just trying to get away from people following him, why not wait for us?"

"He'd know we would come for him," Schiavo said, allowing, at least in part, her medic's supposition.

They were both right. But so was another fact that had begun to occur to me as we searched the lowest decks of the *Vinson*.

"He's been in this situation before," I said.

"What do you mean?" Schiavo pressed me.

"When he was on the hunt for the mole in Bandon during the Unified Government siege," I said. "He was operating in the shadows. We had almost no idea what he was doing until he bagged his quarry."

Private Sheryl Quincy, Schiavo's replacement soldier delivered by the *Rushmore*, had been nothing more than an enemy infiltrator, feeding information to her masters to increase their tactical advantage. And Martin had put a stop to that, working on his own.

"He saw a path to discovery that none of us did, and he followed it," I said. "What if the same situation presented itself when we were scouting the sound on the hangar deck?"

"You think he didn't fall into that hole?" Hart asked.

"I don't know," I said. "If he did or didn't, something down there might have caught his attention."

"And the arrow?" Schiavo asked, referencing the marker Martin had left for us.

"He wanted us to follow him," I said. "We know that. But maybe it's not because he was running, but because he'd found something. Something *he* had to follow—not something he had to run from."

Schiavo processed what I was suggesting. She knew it was well within her husband's makeup to do precisely what I'd described, to spot an opportunity and exploit it.

"We've got to get to the other side, Angela," I said.

It wasn't such a secondary suggestion anymore. Martin had to be beyond the barriers. She looked to her medic.

"You said you have two charges?" she asked.

"Yes, ma'am."

"If my demo training is accurate, two will be just enough," she said. "But not here."

"Where?" I asked.

She jabbed her thumb upward.

"Where we smelled the decomp," she answered.

It was an unpleasant path we would have to take, but it made the most sense.

"We know there was life there recently," I said. "It's gotta lead somewhere."

She nodded and motioned for Hart to get us moving again.

* * *

We reached the intended barrier and were immediately hit by the awful stench slipping through the cracks around the edge.

"Make it happen, Trey," Schiavo ordered.

She and I backed off, taking a position around a corner down the passageway as her medic placed the explosives.

"It makes sense," Schiavo said, looking to me from our position of safety. "That he'd do that."

"I know," I said.

But she shook her head. There was more to her agreement than I was understanding.

"When he gets something in his head," Schiavo began, "some idea or imperative, he becomes a heat-seeking missile. I know he had to be *that* person for so long while leading the town..."

"He wants to protect, Angela."

"He still sees himself as a lone savior sometimes," she said. "Even after I came into his life."

Her frustration was expressed only as some muted feeling. A general desire for him to be different. But I sensed that, inside, where her truest self existed, she was screaming at him right now.

Mostly, though, she was afraid that, because of his actions, she might lose him.

"Ten seconds," Hart said as he came fast around the corner.

He ducked and pressed himself against the same corridor wall we had. I covered my ears and closed my eyes as the seconds ticked down.

Four...
Three...
Two...

Sixteen

BOOM!

The blast pushed a wall of compressed air away from its origin, the wave, mixed with smoke and bits of debris, hitting us even where we'd taken shelter around a corner. It was nowhere near as violent as what I'd experienced just feet from the exploding grenade, seeming almost mild in comparison.

One look around the corner, though, showed the effects were anything but that.

The barrier, just visible through the parting smoke as we moved back into the passageway, had been bent away from us and ripped from its connection to the surrounding walls, just a single corner still attached. The steel slab hung there, shaking still from the explosion, the way past it manageable now.

"They know we're coming," Hart said.

"They've known we were coming before we even landed, Sergeant Hart," Schiavo told him. "But we're not here for a fight. We find Martin, back off, and regroup with the others on the flight deck."

It wasn't a full retreat, but I knew what Schiavo was thinking. Once her husband was safe, we needed to have a better plan now that we knew some adversary with unconventional intentions was aboard. Our tactics, if we were to figure out what threat, if any, the carrier posed to Bandon, would have to be adjusted.

"Let's go get him," I said.

Once more, Hart took the lead, squeezing past the mangled barrier. Schiavo and I followed, the scent of death almost overpowering once we'd entered this new space.

"Every room," Schiavo said. "Fletch and I will check every space, quickly, then move on. You're our cover, Trey."

"Yes, ma'am."

We started moving. I took the right side of the corridor, Schiavo the left. Most compartments were open, their doors pushed back. A few we had to push inward to afford a clear view, each of those moments filled with tense anticipation. We could find anything. But, instead, we found nothing.

Until we reached a watertight door at the end of the corridor we'd followed.

"Cracked open slightly," Hart reported, turning his head slightly from the stench spilling out.

There were no more spaces for Schiavo and I to check. Just the obvious way forward and whatever horror lay beyond.

"I'll take the lead," I said.

Schiavo nodded and I stepped past the medic. I kept my AR in both hands and used my shoulder to move the heavy steel door, stepping over its raised frame as it fully opened. The odor of mass death could almost be felt as I moved forward, like an invisible mist that clung to you as you passed through it. It was overpowering. I coughed, tipping my face against my shoulder.

"I can't breathe," Hart said.

"Focus, Sergeant," Schiavo urged him.

It was difficult to breathe, and the desire to wretch was nearly impossible to resist. My stomach churned, its contents threatening to spill onto the floor.

"Where's it coming from?" I wondered aloud.

"We've just got to get past...past it," Schiavo said.

Martin was our objective. I had to remember that. But knowing where this horror was emanating from was a powerful draw.

That desire was fulfilled when I led us around the corner just ahead.

"Good God..."

The exclamation slipped past my lips without resistance. It was simply impossible to see what I was without reacting.

What had been some sort of recreational space, a gym or gathering room, it appeared, had become the place where dozens had taken their last breaths at the ends of ropes looped over pipes high above.

"How is this possible?" Hart asked.

I had no answer for him, even after a moment of trying to process the sights before us. Each and every person was unclothed, just as the naked man with the grenade had been. There were no bindings on any of them. Their hands and feet were free. In a macabre instant I thought the dozens of bloating corpses filling the space looked like air fresheners dangling from a car's rearview mirror, swaying gently with the motion of the ship.

"Fletch, look," Schiavo said.

She was pointing to a stool, a single stool, tipped over beneath just one of the bodies. The bare feet of each body, depending on the person's height, dangled a foot or two above the floor. Each would have had to be standing on something to place the noose over their head and take their final step.

What Schiavo was pointing out, though, was the chilling manner in which they had done so.

"They took turns," she said. "They all watched the ones before them do it, until the last one was on her own."

It was a woman, I saw. The stool lay on its side directly beneath her. She'd stepped onto it, tightened the noose around her neck, and kicked the support from beneath her.

"Who does something like this?" Hart asked, the incomprehensibility of what he was seeing overpowering the effects of the smell for the moment.

His question, though, was one where some answers existed. Answers with precedence. Mass suicides had, in the past, almost invariably been tied to groups with apocalyptic beliefs. There was another term for them.

"A cult," I said.

Schiavo nodded.

"How many people offed themselves waiting for that spaceship in California?" she asked. "Do you remember that?"

"I do."

"And Jonestown," she said.

Hundreds had consumed poisoned punch in a South American jungle back in the late 70's. I was a child then, but the details of it had persisted in popular culture.

"Angela..."

She looked to me. I gestured toward the body of the woman who'd been the last to end her life in the space.

"You think that's the woman grenade guy was talking about?"

Schiavo didn't have to think on the question. She shook her head.

"That woman was the last in here," she said. "But not the last on board. Leaders of these things are almost always the last to go. They have to make sure their followers stick to the plan. The fact that we've come across living breathing people means this isn't over."

"It is for them," Hart said.

I shifted my position to look through the inverted forest of human shapes.

"There's a door on the far side," I said.

"Trey, are you still keeping track of our position?"

Hart tapped his temple and nodded, the tabletop gamer in him confident.

"Okay, Fletch," Schiavo said, prompting me to get moving again.

I was more than glad to do so. The awful scent, which had been muted by the sights we'd come upon, was making itself prominent again. I stepped past the first group of bodies, weaving carefully between those beyond, trying to avoid any errant contact with the decomposing corpses, making it halfway across the expansive compartment.

Then the lights went out.

Seventeen

In the sudden rush of darkness, too many things happened in rapid succession for us to adequately respond.

The loss of the lighting, which had gone as unexpectedly as it had come, was most jarring. I brought my weapon up and activated its light just as a sound rose. Two sounds, actually. First, the creaking of metallic hinges, from ahead of us it seemed. The door we'd been heading toward had opened. Second was the sound of some impact, hard object striking a harder object. Something landing on the floor nearby, then skidding close to us, just off the right side of our short column.

The beam of my weapon light washed over the door ahead, and I had been correct—the sound I'd heard was it opening. I knew that because I could now see it swinging closed again.

"Grenade!"

The warning came from Schiavo right behind me. I looked fast, instinctively toward where the second sound had come from, off to our right. Enough of the light aimed forward from its mount on my AR had scattered back, revealing a cylindrical explosive not ten feet from us, resting beneath the swaying legs of those who'd already left this life.

I turned my face away just as the device detonated.

The eruption of light and sound far exceeded the concussive effect of the blast, though I was tossed left from the explosion, pinballing off the hanging bodies as brilliant, blinding sparkles overwhelmed my vision. In both ears I heard what I could only describe as a rapid series of thunder cracks, hundreds it seemed. My senses were instantly assaulted by the overwhelming fury of sights and sounds.

My brain, though, was able to craft one clear thought as I fell to the floor—flash bang.

* * *

A hand slapped my face, one cheek then the other. As I began to come out of the daze inflicted upon me by the concussive grenade, I realized several things. My hands were bound behind my back in some sort of wide plastic cuffs, my weapons and vest and backpack were not on or near me, and we were no longer in the room with the hanging bodies.

"Get up," a harsh male voice said.

We were in a hallway, the lights back on, stripped to our boots, pants, and shirts. The smell of decomp and explosive residue hung strong in the air. The room where the flash bang had detonated amongst the bodies had to be adjacent to where I now lay. I shifted my head to scan my surroundings. I could see Schiavo and Hart, sitting against the steel wall, hands bound as mine were, and standing over them were two men wearing black hockey masks, each wielding short barreled M4s.

"Up!"

A hand jerked me off the floor and put me against the wall so that I was reclining as my friends were. I looked up and saw the one who'd manhandled me was armed the same as the others, and wore the same gleaming black mask, his raging gaze wide behind the eye holes.

"Name," the one guarding me demanded.

I hesitated, not out of any desire to resist, but because my brain was still not processing what had happened, and what was happening, at anything approaching a normal pace.

"NAME!" he shouted, putting the stubby barrel of his M4 against my forehead, pinning my skull against the wall. "I'm not asking again."

"Eric Fletcher," I said.

He looked to his comrades and nodded.

"It's him," he said.

It's him...

That implied knowledge of who I was, if not some outright expectation of my presence. The naked man had hinted that our arrival was anticipated. This seemed to be some further confirmation of that.

"This is the garrison commander," one of the other guards said, pointing to Schiavo.

She looked toward me, coming out of the daze as I was.

"What about him?" my captor asked, gesturing toward Hart with his weapon.

"Nobody," the one guarding the medic said.

I didn't like the appraisal that had been offered of Trey Hart. He was not a 'nobody' to us.

"All the way up now," my captor said, and, once more, took hold of me and hauled me upward until I was leaning against the wall.

"I can stand on my own," Schiavo said as her guard reached for her.

She pushed herself off the floor, back sliding up the wall. Next to her, Hart was lifted to a standing position as I was.

"Now, you're going to follow him," the man hovering next to Schiavo said, pointing to his comrade near Hart. "Keep up or we'll make you keep up. We're on a clock."

The one designated to lead us began walking, Hart and Schiavo falling in behind. I took my place next in line, the other two captors trailing me.

We're on a clock...

That could mean many things, I knew. But in light of our situation, it pointed to a most ominous possibility.

A countdown.

Part Three

Project Utopia

Eighteen

We moved along a passageway at gunpoint, our bound hands useless behind us. At the back of our short column, I was urged to move quickly with the collapsed stock of the stubby M4 jabbing me between the shoulder blades. Schiavo was just ahead of me, and Hart in front of her. One of our captors led the way, the other two herding us forward like reluctant cattle.

"Keep moving," the first man behind me said, ramming his weapon into my back again.

I struggled to keep up the pace, the second blast in just a few hours having done a harsh number on my senses. What balance I had was off, and the ringing I'd suffered in my ears had been superseded by a grating, erratic hum. The blinding flash which had washed over us from the concussion grenade had left a constant, painful rain of sparkles dancing across my vision.

"Move!"

Once more the man slammed his rifle stock against my spine, with enough force that I toppled forward, only Schiavo's form keeping me from falling completely. I recovered and forced myself to focus as I walked.

"That's more like it, big man," the vicious captor said to me.

We reached an intersection with another corridor and turned left, coming to a solid, watertight door a few dozen yards down this new passageway. The lead captor stopped us as he thumped the barrier with the edge of his gloved fist.

"We've got them!" he shouted.

A few seconds later the sound of some locking mechanism within the door rose and it swung toward us. Two more masked men stood beyond, each wielding vintage MAC-10 submachineguns which they trained on us as we were moved through the doorway, which was sealed again a few seconds after we passed through.

But we weren't in just some other section of the ship. Something was different here. Had been made different here.

The walls, steel and stout, were not linear like we'd seen throughout the parts of the carrier we'd explored. There was a wide curve to them, with scorch marks every ten feet or so where the large, bent panels had been welded together. It seemed as we progressed further that we were following the outside arc of some circular compartment which had been created deep within the large vessel.

I felt myself slowing again and stumbled, tipping to the right and bouncing off the curved wall. Before another blow was necessary I resumed walking at the pace being set.

"Don't make me thump you again," my captor warned me.

I wasn't going to give him that satisfaction. Every ounce of strength, and every morsel of mental focus I still possessed, I harnessed to stay right behind Schiavo. She glanced over her right shoulder to check on me.

"Eyes forward!" the second man behind me yelled.

It had to burn Schiavo deep within to give in to the command, but she did, not wanting to draw the wrath of our captors on any of us.

The man in the lead stopped and turned to face us, blue eyes peering out through the holes in the hockey mask.

"Lana wants you to see the chamber," he said.

Lana...

Was this the woman the naked man with the grenade had referenced? Logic dictated that it was. But so little of what we'd encountered so far was logical that we couldn't be certain of anything. Except that we were here, at the mercy of armed strangers, on an aircraft carrier whose lower decks were some Frankenstein version of what they'd once been.

"In there," the lead man said, gesturing to an opening in the curved wall. "Walk in and straight across."

Hart stepped forward, slowly, near enough to the opening that an odd glow from within began to hue his face a soft white.

"Holy..."

"Move," the lead captor said as he stayed behind, cutting off any further exclamation from the medic.

Hart stepped into the space, and Schiavo followed. I brought up the rear, and knew immediately why Hart had let the exclamation out.

He had stepped into a jungle.

Or what had been made to mimic a jungle. A path meandered through a wide expanse of earth, whatever fresh smell that might have emanated from it replaced by the scent of stale, lifeless dirt. From it sprouted sickly bushes and drooping palms. Bananas grew on the former, and rotting husks of coconuts lay beneath the latter. Long lines of grape vines hung barren beneath banks of flickering and failing artificial lights high above the manufactured space. More plants, at one time fruit bearing, along with the wilted greens of root vegetables, were spread along once carefully tended rows.

Someone had lovingly, carefully, created this space and tended to it, and had also abandoned it.

"They had blight-proof seeds and plants," I said.

"Quiet," the guard directly behind me ordered, no butt stock between the shoulders added for emphasis this time.

The room was more than a hundred feet long, and forty feet high, covering what had been several decks of the carrier. We continued along the path until we reached another door, two more masked guards standing outside, each armed with what looked to be Benelli semi-auto shotguns.

That choice of weapon reminded me of my friend. Neil had favored the Benelli M1, until he'd lost it in our altercation with the crazed motorcycle gang in Cheyenne. These two, though, they held the fine weapon more like a club, equally ready to bash an enemy with it as to shoot them.

"They're all yours," the guard immediately behind me said.

He stepped past me, and Schiavo, and seized Hart by his collar, dragging him back along the path. Schiavo turned fast to protest, but the taller guard ahead of us grabbed her by the hair and pulled her face close to his mask.

"You don't resist, you don't fight," he told her.

Behind, I could hear Hart being dragged back through the interior jungle. Then, I could hear him no more.

The guard holding Schiavo released her and shoved her back so she bumped into me.

"Listen carefully," the shorter of the two before us said. "In there, you'll give her your full attention. You will only look at her. She is all that matters. Is that clear?"

It wasn't, particularly the 'why' of the directive, but both Schiavo and I nodded.

"Move," the short guard said.

His partner opened the door and we stepped through.

Nineteen

The space was dim, but not blacked out. There was light. One light, and it shone softly from above on a woman seated on the opposite side of a large table a few feet from us.

"Sit," one of our captors said as his partner pulled out two chairs.

Schiavo and I lowered ourselves into the seats and looked across at the dark-haired woman as the men who'd brought us to her withdrew into the shadows.

"My name is Lana," she said.

Lana...

No more than that. And delivered in a crisp feminine voice, accented by time or lineage in some faraway land.

"Where did you take Sergeant Hart?" Schiavo demanded.

"Colonel Schiavo, relax," Lana said. "There is nothing to worry about. Nothing."

"Then tell me where he is," she pressed.

Lana studied Schiavo for a few seconds, sizing up the woman as though contemplating a rival.

"You don't have to do that anymore," Lana said.

"What?"

"Lead," Lana answered.

"We were brought to you," I said, interjecting myself into the exchange. "What do you want from us?"

Now she considered me, though her expression belied that there was no feeling on her part that I was anything approaching an equal.

"You made your way out to my ship," Lana said. "I wasn't going to be rude."

"*Your* ship?" I challenged her.

Once more she focused on me, a hint of displeasure at the flash of insolence I'd expressed toward her.

"Please be mindful of the fact that I could have ordered you shot down," Lana said. "Shot you right out of the air when you first found us. Or when you came back. Or blown your cute little boat out of the water when it came alongside."

"If you park a ship like this near us and announce your presence, you have to expect a visit," I said. "You weren't that hard to find."

Her shoulders shrugged slightly, not agreeing or disagreeing with my statement.

"For you, maybe," she said, her gaze shifting between Schiavo and me. "For others, the few that there are, I'm not so sure. There's something...special about you. About Bandon. You're..."

She had difficulty dredging whatever word she sought from her lexicon.

"Resilient," I said.

"Defiant," Schiavo added.

Lana considered that, then shook her head.

"It's more than that. You're all so...precious."

Schiavo and I glanced at each other, then looked back to Lana, who seemed to be stifling a chuckle.

"You all still believe," the woman said, a quiet exasperation filling her now.

"In ourselves? We absolutely do," I said.

Behind us a door opened and a young man, no older than Carter Laws appeared, walking past us and around the table with a tray in hand. From it he set a plate of food and a glass of red wine in front of Lana before withdrawing, not a word or a look exchanged between them. The door closed again with a heavy metallic *clunk* a few seconds later.

"Thank you, Nicholas," she thanked the servant in his absence. "Dinner time."

She began to eat, cutting into one of the juiciest steaks I'd seen in ages. Between bites she drank from the rich burgundy beverage in her glass.

"It's a shame you can't taste any of this," she said as she continued feasting.

"What about them?" I asked, chancing a glance behind into the shadows where her guards had withdrawn.

"I wouldn't do that," she admonished, pausing with a forked piece of meat near her lips.

In that darkness behind Schiavo and me I heard a hushed rustle. The sound of a weapon being raised. Our hockey-masked captors were apparently deadly serious about their duties.

"Fletch..."

Schiavo's soft warning drew my attention back toward Lana.

"Where was I before this delicious repast was delivered?" she asked, drinking and thinking for a moment. "Right...*belief.*"

She almost spat the word as us, putting the fork and knife down next to the unfinished steak, keeping the glass in hand as she considered us with a harsh, almost hateful pity.

"Believing got us all to where we are," she said. "Believing in God, in government, in humanity."

"So you believe in nothing," Schiavo said.

"Of course I do," Lana said. "I believe in the end."

"The end of what?" Schiavo asked.

"Us," Lana answered, sipping her wine again.

I understood right then. Understood what she was, if not who she was. An apocalypse freak. One who'd likely reveled in the appearance of the blight, and who'd marveled gleefully at the devastation it had wrought.

"Your accent," I said. "You're not American."

"No," she said, shaking her head slowly. "I am not."

"Where are you from?" I pressed.

"It's that vague European manner about me, isn't it?" she asked, not expecting, nor waiting for, any reply. "The edged tone and the subtle lilt in my voice."

I thought for a moment on what she'd said, and how she'd said it. The subdued accent was hard to pin down, but, when taken with what she'd revealed and what we'd all learned about the origins of the blight, a realization rose quickly.

"You're Polish," I said.

She smiled.

"You're very observant," she said. "Or is it intuitive? Did you guess, or did you know?"

"You were there," I said, sidestepping her counter questioning. "When it started, you were there."

"More than that," she replied, coyly withholding further explanation.

"How so?" Schiavo asked, joining the almost genial probing.

"I was just a girl who took a walk in a potato field near Warsaw and emptied a vial," she said.

"You," Schiavo said, the accusation almost breathless.

"You worked with Borgier," I said.

Borgier. The French Foreign Legion officer who'd developed a cult of personality. Who'd groomed a cadre of soldiers and followers who worshipped him. He'd bankrolled and protected the Iraqi scientist who'd developed the blight, and its human equivalent, BA-412. That he was actually an American named Gray Jensen was no secret.

"He thought I did," Lana said. "I suppose we both had our motives. His mistake was believing that he could gain power through the chaos that would come."

"And you?" Schiavo asked.

"We had hopes," Lana said, then sipped from her glass, the deep burgundy wine disappearing past her lips. "Misplaced as they were."

"Hopes?" I asked, almost past caring what the woman had to say.

She finished what remained of the wine and put the delicate glass down, staring at me for a moment with a grin that reeked of disdain. And pity.

"What?" I pressed her.

"Four Twelve," she said.

Four Twelve...

How many times had I heard that number? That term. And what it represented. Where one had wiped out all plant life on the planet, the other would have done the same to what was left of the human population.

Those simple arrangement of digits and letters tied me inexorably to my friend. To Neil. He, though, had apparently hidden the only sample of that virus somewhere without telling a soul how to find it.

Not even me.

"We couldn't obtain it," Lana said, hinting at disappointment for the first time since we'd been face to face with her.

"You wanted to release it," I said. "The blight was only the appetizer to you."

"It doesn't matter anymore," Lana said, almost dismissive, as if the exchange between us had run its course from curiosity to tedium. "A handful scattered here and there. Twenty in Australia, a hundred across the whole of Russia."

"We have estimates that there are millions left," I told her.

Lana shook her head.

"Your estimates are wrong," she said. "Fewer than twenty thousand living, breathing human beings are left."

That number would have comprised a medium-sized town in the old world. Now, she was saying that was it.

"You have no way of knowing who's alive and where," I said.

"Do you know what I did before all this?" Lana asked. "What I did when I met Borgier? I was director of the United Nations Permanent Committee on Population and Sustainability."

A U.N. bureaucrat. How appropriate, I thought. A functionary with apocalyptic ideals embedded within a world body that, prior to the blight, had become an institution riddled by corruption and fecklessness.

"Borgier had many contacts with people in positions of power," Lana said. "So, yes, I used his openness to authority to my own ends."

She'd played the role of some double agent for her own purposes. Siding with Borgier to gain access to the blight. She might have even urged him to deploy it, and volunteered to be the one to release its hell upon the world. All this to curry his favor in hopes of acquiring the even more devastating BA-412 virus.

"If you're throwing out your involvement with the United Nations to sound legitimate," Schiavo began, "don't bother."

"An exclusive club of the global elite who pulled strings for the benefit of a very few," Lana said, nailing what many had come to believe about the once promising organization. "I can confirm that is quite true."

"Is that damning praise?" Schiavo challenged her.

"No," Lana answered. "It's just that you might want to know that I was as surprised as you when the whole damn thing actually began to function as it had been intended once the world started to crumble. These petty men, and most of them were men, they coalesced around finding some way to recover from the blight. And one thing necessary to that goal was determining exactly where the survivors were."

"A census," I said.

"Exactly," Lana confirmed. "We worked on that even as the numbers still working at the United Nations dwindled. As staff and those they served succumbed, to famine or the bouts of violence that swept every capital. Every major city."

"Every minor city, as well," I remined her.

"Which made a survey by ground impossible," she said. "Most was done by air, through satellite imagery, or government knowledge. One place, through all this, its name kept coming up—Bandon. This quaint little town on the American west coast where people were *actually* making it. Where the population was increasing. Everywhere else, it was the reverse. Where everywhere else death was the norm, life came to your town. It flourished. Even when obstacle after obstacle came your way."

She regarded that fact for a moment with subtle wonder.

"You became known among what passed for world leaders," Lana said. "Praise was lavished on you from afar. Supplies were sent to assist you."

She picked up the empty wine glass and tipped it over, a few drops of the beverage dripping out.

"That's all over now, thankfully," she said.

"What do you mean?" Schiavo asked.

Lana smiled, withholding for effect.

"You said over," Schiavo pressed. "What's over?"

The woman stood from where she'd sat, just stood, not moving, the table with her mostly finished meal between us. It seemed to me a statement, the posture she took. She was free to rise. We were not. The shotguns pointed at our backs from the shadows enforced that.

"Your delivery service has been terminated," Lana said, still smiling.

"The *Rushmore*," I said. "You sank it."

She chuckled now, mostly to herself.

"That's funny?" I challenged her.

"Your limited imagination is," she told me.

"Enlighten us," Schiavo said, more than a hint of a challenge in her words.

"You think that you're alive because of the *Rushmore*?" Lana asked, part incredulous, and part angry. "You really believe that some resupply chain has kept you going?"

"It hasn't hurt," I said.

She shook her head at my quip.

"You're alive, all of you, *because* of all of you," she said, as if leveling a heinous charge against us. "You're thriving. You're growing. You're the seed that humanity regenerates from."

She settled back into her chair, her expression gone slack.

"And that can't be allowed to happen."

Her motives, and the end game associated with them, were beginning to come into focus. And she was now more than happy to let us in on what the future held. What *our* future, or lack thereof, held.

"Two ships were loaded with the movable weapons from the strategic stockpile of the United States of America," Lana explained. "Two carriers. The *Eisenhower* and the *Vinson*. The powers that be at the time didn't want any of these bombs and spare warheads just lying around for the taking once everything went to hell. The ICBMS and the subs were secure enough, they figured. But the things that could be loaded on a truck, or van, or an aircraft...that spooked them."

"So they put them on a pair of carriers to sail around until things calmed down," I said. "That's what you're saying?"

She stood again, moving this time, walking around the table to a place where she leaned against its edge, closest to me.

"Yes," she confirmed.

"And you gained control," I said. "Just like that."

She savored my doubt for a moment. It seemed to nourish her sense of superiority. She knew things, and we didn't. Parceling out morsels was her power play.

Along with having control of a nuclear-powered aircraft carrier.

"Eric, how many people do you think sailed on this ship when it began its final mission? It would normally have over five thousand, but how many were present for this most momentous voyage?"

"I have no idea," I told her.

"Seventy-three," Lana said, cocking her head a bit to appraise my appreciation of that number. "A skeleton crew. And among those, Eric, how many do you think had it in their heads that the cause was already lost? That we'd finally gotten what was coming to us as a species after what we'd done to each other, and to this beautiful planet?"

Like minds, I thought. That was what she was talking about. It was how she, and her ilk, had taken control of the *Vinson* and, if she was being truthful, the strategic weaponry it held.

"Seven," Lana said, answering her own question. "Ten percent of the crew. I wasn't aboard then, but it must have been a beautiful thing to witness those brave sailors dispatch their brethren. The other vessel was similarly taken."

At that moment, it would have been most appropriate to blurt out *'You're mad!'* But, other than the dramatics of doing so, there was no point. Whether she was insane didn't matter. She'd staked out an insane position, adopting the ideology that the human presence on earth had become caustic.

"I came aboard over a year ago," Lana said. "Just off the eastern coast of South America. That was when we began our preparations. Which you saw on your way in. We built our own little utopia in the bowels of this ship to sustain us until our final victory. The *Eisenhower* was prepared in the same way."

"Your utopia is dying," Schiavo said.

"Everything does," Lana agreed.

"Like all those people we found at the end of ropes?" I asked.

Lana drew a breath, considering something, it seemed, then she stepped away from where she'd come and returned to her place on the opposite side of the table. She did not sit, though.

"Have Nicholas come back in," she said past us.

The door opened, and thirty seconds later closed again. The young man who'd served her approached and stood facing Lana.

"Nicholas, are you ready?" she asked him.

The bottom suddenly fell out of my stomach.

No...

"I am," Nicholas told her.

"Are you sure?" she probed. "You choose the time."

"This is my time," he assured her.

Lana smiled and nodded and reached behind her back, retrieving a compact, stainless steel pistol. She held it out and Nicholas took it.

"Don't," Schiavo said, sensing exactly what I was.

The young man looked at the weapon, then ensured that a round was chambered. He thumbed the safety off and took two steps back from Lana before tipping his head back, opening his mouth, and slipping the barrel in.

Both Schiavo and I let our gazes settle on the tabletop as the young man pulled the trigger. The thud of his body hitting the floor announced that he had joined the others who'd ended their lives aboard the *Vinson*.

"There," Lana said.

Schiavo and I looked up.

"That's barbaric," Schiavo said. "He was almost a child."

"He was ready to go," Lana said, sitting again. "Soon the rest of us will join him and the others."

"The others," Schiavo said. "Like the ones dead at the end of ropes? Or blown up by their own hand?"

"Or gunned down by you?" Lana prompted, smiling.

"You sent them after us knowing they'd lose," Schiavo said. "They were just fodder."

We stared at her, knowing exactly what the grand plan was now. What *her* grand plan was now.

I also realized what she'd already done.

"The *Eisenhower* sailed to Hawaii," I said. "Didn't it?"

Westin had reported that some burst of energy had been detected at a great distance. Hawaii, the distribution point of our supplies, lay far from Bandon in the middle of the Pacific Ocean.

Or it had.

"You didn't just sink the *Rushmore*," I said. "You blew up the islands."

"A few dozen megatons will do that," Lana said.

The purpose of what we'd experienced also began to fall into place.

"You had to keep us from talking to Hawaii," I said.

Schiavo let out a shallow breath, the realization hitting her as well.

"If they report the arrival of a carrier, and then we lose contact, your presence would draw a response," Schiavo theorized.

"We couldn't have you spot us and do some kamikaze run with an explosive-filled plane," Lana said. "Sinking us a hundred miles off shore would be such a waste. But..."

"But what?" I pressed her.

She eyed us with wonder, I thought, a not entirely antagonistic look upon her face.

"But I did think it would also bring you to me," Lana said.

We'd been right about our belief behind what the naked man with the grenade had said before ending his life. Someone had foretold our arrival. A woman. This woman.

"I wanted so much to meet you both," she said. "Your names were always among those mentioned when the powers that be discussed why Bandon had survived. Just...seeing you, it explains so much. Except..."

"Except what?" Schiavo asked.

"I'm surprised he didn't come with you," Lana said.

"Who?"

She answered my question with a reply neither Schiavo or I could have anticipated.

"Martin Jay," Lana said. "He was the architect of Bandon's survival, and I didn't think he'd let his loving wife out of his sight."

Schiavo didn't react. Neither did I. What the woman had just let us know, through a simple statement of ignorance, was that Martin had not been taken by them. And, more important, they didn't seem to be aware that he had come aboard with us.

"So you've seen us," I said, speaking before Schiavo would have to. "What happens now?"

"What happens now is that you get the best seat in the house," Lana said. "When we sail to Bandon, you will be the very first to witness the end. It won't register, of course. We're talking milliseconds. But up until that very fraction of a second, you will know what's about to transpire before your eyes."

"You're going to wipe out our town," I said. "Because you want the world to end?"

"Eric, Angela, if you haven't realized it by now, you never will," Lana said.

"What?" Schiavo asked, humoring the calm and crazed woman.

"That *we* are the blight on this planet," Lana answered. "Humanity. People. And we always have been."

She looked past us, into the shadows, and nodded. The two masked men who guarded us came forward and pulled us up out of our chairs.

"We won't be seeing each other again," Lana said. "Mother nature needs a clean slate."

Schiavo eyed her for a second, glaring at the apparent architect of Bandon's final destruction.

"Go to hell," Schiavo said.

Lana didn't react, but the guards did, jerking us roughly away from the table and marching through the shadows to the door.

Twenty

A minute later, after passing through the wasting space that had served as some kind of greenhouse, Schiavo and I were pushed face first against the wall of a corridor and ordered to be silent. One of the two men guarding us told his partner to keep a watch on us while he retrieved the key. Whatever key he meant, and whichever lock it might be for, I didn't care. For a moment, we outnumbered the people who had taken us.

"Can you get out of the cuffs?" I whispered to Schiavo, angling my gaze along the wall to see her reaction.

She shook her head slightly, almost imperceptibly. I'd tried already to wrench my wrists up and through the plastic bindings, to no avail. Now any hope that Schiavo might be able to do what I hadn't was gone.

"She's lying," Schiavo said in a hushed tone. "She didn't hope the signal would bring us out here. She needed it to."

"Why?"

"The same reason she expected Martin to be with us," Schiavo answered. "To get as many decision makers out of the equation as possible."

"Why not just sail the *Vinson* in without warning and detonate?" I wondered quietly, my breathy words hot against the cold steel wall before me.

"What if one of the fishing boats spots them?" Schiavo theorized. "Or a flight? Or the *Rushmore* coming from Hawaii?"

I understood now what she was saying.

"It had to be coordinated and we had to be in the blind," I said.

"Quiet!"

The order came sharp from behind, and a few seconds later the guard who'd left returned. He and his partner pulled us away from the wall and pushed us so that we were ahead of them in the corridor.

"Walk," the one directly behind us ordered.

We did, moving through the ship, following the directions of our two captors, travelling down steps and along passageways. Making our way toward a place where Lana had said we would be the first to witness the hell she had planned. There was only one place that could be—where the nukes were.

I flashed back to what the President had shown us on the upper floors of the skyscraper in Columbus. That was a single weapon, with 400 kilotons of explosive energy, would be dwarfed by what was carried by the *Vinson*.

If Lana wasn't lying.

There was no reason to believe that she was. No benefit existed for her, or her apocalyptic vision, if bluff and bluster was all she wielded. Our lives could be ended at any moment by those who followed her orders, but an empty vessel sailing toward Bandon would be of no strategic value—unless it held exactly what she claimed.

"Straight ahead," the nearest guard behind me said as we came around a corner.

There was no point in attempting any resistance. We couldn't. Not at the moment. When we reached where they were leading us...maybe. It might be our last stand, but at least we would be taking one.

As it turned out, someone else took that stand for us.

Twenty One

The shots came from behind us. Two. Schiavo and I dropped to the floor when the first rang out, hearing a thud and the metallic clunk of a weapon falling behind us. The second shot rang out almost immediately, the same pair of sounds following. Bodies and guns had hit the floor of the passageway.

But not our bodies.

We looked behind and saw both guards lying in heaps, blood gushing from massive head wounds in each. And beyond them, crouched low just outside a compartment we'd passed only seconds before, was Martin, M4 in hand, wisps of smoke rising from its barrel.

"Martin..."

Schiavo's relief, her joy, was softened only by the surprise at what had just happened. At who we were seeing.

"Let's get you out of those," Martin said.

He slung his rifle and stepped past the bodies as we stood. He used a knife to cut the plastic cuffs from our wrists. As soon as she was free, Schiavo put her arms around her husband.

"You have a hell of a lot of explaining to do," she told him as she clutched him in her embrace.

"I've got plenty to tell," he said. "But we have to move, first."

I crouched and took the guards' shotguns in hand, keeping one for myself and handing the other to Schiavo as she eased back from Martin.

That was when we both noticed the blood covering the front of his shirt and gear vest. Lots of blood.

"Are you hurt?" I asked.

"No," he assured us. "I'll explain. But we've got to get away from this."

"Sergeant Hart was with us," Schiavo said, worried about yet another missing member of our group. "He's got to be back with that woman."

"Woman?" Martin asked.

I took a brief moment to explain who, and what, we'd witnessed. When I was done he nodded, as if relieved he'd been handed pieces of some nagging puzzle.

"This is all making more sense now," Martin said.

"We have to go back," Schiavo told him, bringing the semi-auto shotgun up to a low ready position.

To that order, Martin shook his head.

"Trey's not back there," he said.

"What do you mean?" Schiavo pressed him. "Where is he?"

"Follow me," Martin said.

He led off, favoring his left leg.

"You *are* hurt," Schiavo said.

"Dropping through a hole in the floor isn't good on the ankles," Martin told us.

He had fallen through, exactly as we'd suspected. And he'd survived. And he'd saved us.

Now, all we had to do was save everyone else that we knew and loved.

* * *

Martin took us along a maze-like path through the corridors that cut across the length of the lower deck we'd been taken to.

"There," Martin said, gesturing with a nod.

A watertight door lay ahead, slightly open, and just outside it to one side of it a body was piled against the corridor's wall, a pool of blood spread beneath it. For an instant I saw Schiavo's color go ashen. But just for an instant. Almost immediately she realized that her worst fear at the moment had not been realized—Martin had not led us to Hart's body.

"He was guarding that door," Martin explained. "I had to use the knife. Gunshots echo through this ship, from deck to deck. And explosions."

"We've been up close to a couple of those," I said.

"That's what I was afraid of when I heard them."

"Why did you take off?" Schiavo asked him, more than a hint of impatience in her question.

"Right after I fell, there was movement outside the compartment where I landed," he said. "Three armed men. They passed by without looking."

"Hockey masks?" I asked.

Martin shook his head.

"Helmets and top notch gear," he said.

"Like the ones who tried to hit us on the hangar deck," Schiavo said.

"They weren't pros," Martin said.

"Neither were the ones we took out," I told him.

"I knew I could either fight, maybe with an advantage because I'd be behind them, or..."

"Or you could follow them," Schiavo said.

"There's only one way that connects this part of the ship to the side they cut off with those welded walls," Martin said. "I know where it is."

"So we can get back to the others," I said.

Schiavo reached out and tapped her husband firmly on one shoulder.

"Where is Trey?"

Once more Martin motioned to the door. This time, though, he stepped toward it and leaned close to the narrow gap between it and the steel frame that surrounded it.

"We're coming in, Trey," he said.

The door swung inward, pulled from within. We stepped through and Sergeant Trey Hart, wielding a shotgun caked with dried blood from the dispatched guard, stood at the ready.

"Good to see you again, ma'am."

Schiavo stepped close and put a relieved hand on her soldier's arm.

"You, too, Trey."

Martin closed the door behind, sealing it completely now, cranking an interior lever which locked it in a full watertight position.

"Angela," I said, noticing a series of chains looped over a thick pipe that ran high along the wall of the large space, handcuffs at each end.

"I think these were for us," I said.

"And that's for everyone else," Hart said, pointing to a stack of grey crates that bisected the room, a narrow way past on one end. "On the other side."

Schiavo went first, Martin and I right behind as Hart remained to cover the door. It only took us a minute to make it to the other side.

Lana, as I'd suspected, was not lying. At all.

Twenty Two

The bombs and warheads rested in steel racks, with electrical cables snaking from each to a central control box that was welded to the deck.

"This look familiar to you, Fletch?"

I knew what Schiavo was referencing. The sandbagged upper floor of the skyscraper in Columbus, Ohio. There the President of the United States had shown us one weapon.

This was not one weapon.

"Times fifty," I said. "Maybe sixty."

That's how many weapons I estimated were held in the latticework of steel supports.

"Armored elevator to the hangar deck is back beyond them," Martin said.

"Let me guess," I said. "Welded shut."

He nodded.

"They brought them down and sealed them in," he said.

"Just like they sealed themselves in," Schiavo added.

"I don't imagine that just cutting all this wiring would disarm these," I said.

"That's not a chance we can take," Schiavo said.

It was the cliché—the red wire or the green wire. Or the white wire. Or any wire. The truth was, we had none of the required skillset necessary to even consider attempting what I was wondering about.

"Can these all be detonated simultaneously?" Martin asked. "Won't one going off destroy the others before they can go boom?"

Schiavo stepped close to the collection of megatonnage and put a hand on one of the bomb casings.

"More than one won't be necessary if this ship gets close to Bandon," she said, looking to me and Martin. "We can't let that happen."

"Agreed," I said, lifting the shotgun I'd acquired up for display. "We won't do it with these."

"I know," Schiavo said, turning to her husband next. "Can you get us to the flight deck?"

He shook his head.

"Hangar deck," he said.

Schiavo accepted that limitation with a nod.

"We'll rope it from there," she said.

* * *

A few minutes later we were in line behind Martin, following his lead along corridors and up steep stairs, some of which we'd traversed while cuffed and under guard. The further we progressed, the clearer it became to me that we were nearing the starboard side of the *Vinson*. Soon after that realization I felt the cool wash of ocean air.

"Through here," Martin said.

He pushed the door to a compartment open, revealing a narrow opening to some sort of balcony hanging over the water.

"We have to be just below the island," Hart said, his map keeping skills estimating our location.

"Two decks below," Martin said. "But all access into the island is blocked. This is the only way to move up. There's another balcony adjacent to this one. Maybe a five-foot gap. We just have to cross, step inside, and there's a short set of stairs up to the hangar deck. It lets out behind a wall in the shadows. I'd imagine that's how the ones who tried to hit you got access."

I stepped to the edge of the space, where solid flooring ended and the steel mesh balcony began. In the weak starlight I could barely make out the next balcony over, just as Martin had described it. Above, running from one to the other, a pipe was mounted on thick supports.

"You can use that for balance," Martin said, noting where my attention had shifted.

Below, the ocean churned, slapping the side of the *Vinson* with ten-foot waves, rocking the ship. Any hand or foothold would be precarious. But it appeared to be our only way back to the rest of our group, and to our way off the carrier.

"Sergeant Hart, secure that door," Schiavo ordered.

Hart did that, stepping back to cover the entrance. Schiavo looked to Martin and me.

"Who's first?"

Martin stepped past me.

"I've done it already with a bum leg," he said. "And come back."

"You cross and spot the rest of us," Schiavo said.

Martin slung his M4 and hopped awkwardly onto the waist-high railing that surrounded the small balcony, which now appeared to be some access to the exterior of the carrier for maintenance purposes. He pushed with his uninjured leg and gripped the pipe above, using his hold on it to pendulum his body across the short distance to the other balcony. When he had one foot planted solidly on its railing, he slid his hands along the pipe until he was in a position to jump down.

"That's all it is," Martin said once he landed on the balcony floor.

"Sergeant Hart..."

The medic heeded his commander's call and took his turn crossing over as I maintained a watch on the door.

"They're not coming after us," I said.

"She's running out of live bodies to do her dirty work," Schiavo suggested as Hart reached to the pipe overhead.

I looked to the door again, unnerved by the truth of what Schiavo had said.

"Angela..."

"What, Fletch?"

"If she's out of people, who's going to sail this ship toward shore?"

Schiavo didn't react, but I knew that she hadn't considered that very simple requirement of finishing what she'd started.

"She's gotta have a crew to do that," I added.

"Maybe she does," Schiavo suggested.

More people hidden away, waiting for their turn to serve the greater purpose. It was possible, I thought, but something didn't feel right about that. Lana hadn't seemed worried about our presence as a force to stop her, which we would have a chance to do by eliminating those waiting to crew the *Vinson*.

"Something's not right," I said, looking to the door once more.

Hart finished crossing and stood next to Martin. Schiavo looked to me, my turn at hand.

"Fletch, we can't analyze her plan right now," she told me. "We've gotta get back with the others."

I only hesitated a second, then climbed onto the railing, tossed my shotty over to Martin, and reached for the pipe.

That was when the rogue wave struck the carrier, thirty feet of foaming water that slammed into the starboard bow, shifting the position and angle of the handhold I was reaching for. I missed and slipped, my body tipping forward and away from the ship.

"Fletch!"

Martin called out to me at the same time he reached for my falling body. I was groping for his outstretched hand at the same instant.

And I missed.

There was only water below me. And no hope of avoiding a certainly fatal fall into it. That's what I believed in that split second. But I was wrong. The solid grip suddenly circling my right ankle made that wonderfully clear.

It was Schiavo. She'd seized my leg and prevented me from plunging into the swirling sea. Instead, my body pitched forward and swung, smashing into the railing, upside down.

"I've got you," Schiavo assured me.

I grabbed the bottom of the railing, my injured finger afire as I gripped the handhold, and twisted my upper body back toward safety, getting my free leg back onto the edge of the balcony. The *Vinson* continued to pitch wildly as I climbed back over the railing and stood next to Schiavo.

"That's the way not to do it," I said.

"Thanks for the demonstration," Schiavo said, allowing a nervous chuckle.

I attempted the crossing again, successfully this time, with Martin ready to steady me against the ship's motion. After I was safely across, Schiavo followed, her husband and I both giving her an assist to ensure there were no more near misses.

I glanced to the other balcony we'd just left, and the opening to the interior of the ship. No one was coming after us. I'd told Schiavo just moments before that something wasn't right. I felt that more strongly now.

"Fletch..."

Schiavo called to me from the opening to the ship's interior. Martin and Hart were already inside, making their way to the stairs Martin had earlier discovered. We were leaving Lana's lair behind.

But I had a terrible feeling that we hadn't left it behind for good.

Twenty Three

The stairs led to the hangar deck as Martin said they would. As in the rest of the ship, lights had been selectively reactivated, though only a few burned in the vast space beneath the flight deck, hardly enough to reveal much.

Except our position.

"The rope's still there," I said.

The faint light was enough to show that the rope we'd rappelled down, and which Westin and Laws had ascended, still swung from its anchor point, whipping about in the open elevator well. We had to get to it to reach our friends, *and* our only way off the carrier. Doing so would require a dash across the open space.

"A lot of shadows out there," Hart commented.

There were. In recesses along the hangar deck's outer wall, anyone could be hiding.

"Another ambush?" Schiavo wondered, looking to me.

I shook my head. Despite my uneasy feelings about our seemingly unmolested escape, a second attack on us here, on the hangar deck, seemed illogical.

"If she wanted to she could hit us up top," I said. "With everyone and the plane vulnerable."

"She has the run of the ship," Martin said, adding credence to my observation.

"Move and cover," Schiavo said, nodding to her medic to take the lead.

Hart rose from the cover we'd taken and jogged across the hangar deck, positioning himself near the edge of the aircraft elevator where he secured the swinging rope with one hand and covered our continuing advance with the rifle in his other.

Martin went next, running with difficulty, his injury slowing him down appreciably.

"You're tail gunner again," Schiavo said.

I nodded and she headed out across the space just as Martin reached cover. Once she was safely with the others, I rose and ran, scanning the shadows and glancing behind, wary of some ambush that, in other situations, would be almost certain given the lay of the land. None came, though, and I reached the elevator, taking the slack end of the rope from Hart.

"I'll cover topside and get help to haul Martin up," I said.

"Sorry about the bum leg," he said.

He didn't want to be a burden on anyone, but there was no way he could use the rope to walk himself up the side of the elevator well.

"Have you up in no time," I told Martin.

The shotgun I'd acquired, a Benelli M1, had no sling attached to it. Ignoring most rules of proper handling, I made sure the safety was on and slid the long weapon between my belt and pants, securing it as one might a sword in a scabbard. Then I gripped the rope and pulled myself up, planting my boots on the steel wall and creeping upward, hands pulling, feet walking, the broken and bandaged finger almost an afterthought now. Within a minute I was at the edge of the elevator well where it met the flight deck. A small recess there allowed me to slip one boot in for a foothold while I brought my shotgun back up and peered over the edge.

We had no way of knowing if any of our friends were still there, but when I peered across the wide landing strip I could see, in the weak glow of lights which had come on like those below, Carter Laws and Chris Beekman crouching near the corner of the jamming structure, weapons at the ready.

I hauled myself fully onto the flight deck and crouched low.

"Hey!" I shouted, loud enough to cut through the constant wind buffeting the ship and screaming across the deck.

Carter and Beekman looked at the same instant, weapons swiveling. Both, fortunately, were able to see that it was not an enemy calling to them, but a friend. The Corporal signaled for the pilot to stay with the plane, then he jogged across the deck to where I'd appeared.

"Fletch."

"It's good to see you, Carter," I said, scanning the space beyond him once more. "Where's Ed?"

"He got into the island," Carter said, pointing to the superstructure rising on the starboard side of the ship. "He's working on the radio. Should I get him?"

I shook my head. Schiavo had charged Sergeant Ed Westin with establishing some sort of communications link with Bandon. That was vital. Carter and I could manage what needed to be done at the elevator, leaving Beekman to guard the Cessna.

"Give me a hand," I told Carter.

Five minutes later we had Hart, Schiavo and Martin on the flight deck. We crossed it with Carter, the first licks of rain from a building storm starting to fall.

"The plane is good?" Schiavo asked.

"The plane is fine," Beekman assured her. "We felt an explosion."

The blast which we'd set off to gain access to Lana's section of the ship had been transmitted through the structure, alerting our friends, as well as her people, that we had breached their barrier.

"That was us," I said said, nearly toppling over when the ship rolled hard with a wave.

I took a moment to update Beekman on what had transpired below. When I was done, he looked across the rainy deck and clutched his compact shotgun a bit more tightly.

"I'm ready to get off this ship asap," he said.

"Join the club," I agreed.

A few yards away, Martin stumbled as Schiavo talked with Corporal Wells and Sergeant Hart. I hurried over and helped him to a position under the Cessna's wing, partly shielded from the elements. He leaned against the fuselage and took his weight off the offending limb.

"You think it's broken?" I asked, gesturing to his ankle.

He shook his head.

"Did that when I was nineteen and invincible on a dirt bike," he shared. "Different feeling. It's just twisted. I banged it up good."

"You know, that took some guts," I said. "What you did down there."

Martin shrugged off the praise.

"I was trying to reach a better position when I saw those guys moving on you and Angela. That hole swallowed me before I knew it."

"Still," I said.

He understood that I was trying to be both complimentary, and thankful. He'd saved us down there, and his covert scouting had allowed us to return to where we now stood.

"Fletch..."

It was Schiavo. She motioned me over as Hart and Laws moved to positions to secure more of the flight deck.

"Give that ankle a rest," I told Martin, then joined Schiavo.

"Join me in the island," she requested.

Westin was in there, according to Carter Laws. Working whatever magic he could with the remnants of the carrier's communications system.

"Let's go," I said.

It was vital that he succeed, I knew. And I suspected why that was so, considering what Schiavo might do with the ability to communicate should Westin be able to provide that to her.

Twenty Four

We found Westin several levels up in the island, the upper half of his body twisted into the space beneath a console he'd pried open.

"I'm close, I think," he told us as we waited. "Just a minute more."

"I'm counting on you, Ed," Schiavo said, her words praising and prodding at the same time.

I looked around the space, a few lights on here. It seemed to me that the job Lana's people had done on the carrier had left some spaces with only dim emergency lighting, and other areas, such as those she controlled, with a full complement of illumination. I wondered if that was going to be a problem for the garrison's com expert.

"Do you have power in there?" I asked.

"Just enough amps," Westin answered, his reply muffled somewhat by thin steel panels and bundles of unused cables still stuffing the electronics cabinet.

Similar metal boxes were arranged along the outer wall of what must have been the bridge. Commands were given here, at one time, to guide the ship. To steer it into ports. Or into war.

Now, though, the majority of the floor space was bare. Where navigation consoles and controls had once been located, only severed conduits remained, poking up from the floor. There was no ship's wheel for steering. No chair for the captain. Someone had either moved those things to a different part of the vessel, for use there, or they'd simply wanted to remove all ability to control the carrier from this space.

Westin finished and wriggled his way out of the space beneath the console, unspooling a length of coaxial cable with him. He passed one end up to me and stood, hunching over the radio he'd brought along, removing its antenna and attaching the end of the cable to it.

"Will it work?" Schiavo pressed him.

"I'm tapping into the ship's antenna array," the com specialist said. "But I have no way of knowing which array. It could be HF or UHF or..."

He wasn't certain. Worse, he was worried that he was failing his commander.

"Ed," Schiavo said, and the sergeant looked to her. "You're doing your best."

Westin accepted the reassurance with a nod.

"We're getting some power from the ship, but I don't know how much will match to our output," Westin said.

"Meaning?" I asked him.

"Meaning we could transmit a thousand miles skipping off the atmosphere, or two hundred yards to the end of the flight deck."

Schiavo reached out and he passed the handheld radio to her to her.

"We'll know soon enough," Schiavo said, then glanced to me.

Normally it would be Schiavo asking her subordinate to leave a space so that matters above his pay grade could be discussed. She'd very openly delegated that task to me. Westin didn't understand why, but I did. She wanted me there because I was already a party to what was to come.

Viper Diamond Nine...

"Ed, can you give us the room," I said.

"And ask Martin to come up," Schiavo added.

Through one of the thick windows angled down toward the flight deck, I could glimpse Martin standing awkwardly with Beekman and the other two members of the garrison who'd come to the carrier. All stood at the ready, guarding the plane, Martin still taking the weight off his injured leg by leaning against the fuselage. The Cessna was our lifeline to civilization. To Bandon. Without it...

Without it we would die at sea along with anyone left on the carrier.

"Will do," Westin said, then he hustled off the bridge.

"It's only one-thirty," I said.

Schiavo nodded. The sub, if it still existed, was supposed to be listening for our call at 3 in the morning or 3 in the afternoon. We were 90 minutes shy of the former.

"To hell with the clock," Schiavo said. "Someone has to be monitoring the radio."

After years of waiting for a call that, to this point, had not come, and might never come, would any surviving members of the sub's crew be listening at an off hour? And, if they were, would they heed our call at this time?

"How long is the flight to Bandon, Fletch?"

I did some quick calculations, and added those to my recollections of the nearly completed round trip I'd made with Chris Beekman.

"Figure an hour and fifteen minutes," I said. "Give or take."

"Say an hour and a half to be safe," Schiavo said. "A three-hour round trip. That gives us three hours."

The 'us' she'd said included me, I knew. And likely Martin, as well.

"I'm sending my guys back on the first flight with Beekman," she said.

"And us?" I asked.

"We wait," she said.

"Wait for what?"

We looked toward the entrance to the bridge and saw Martin standing there, M4 slung. He hobbled toward us, supporting himself with handholds on the battered consoles which had once aided in controlling the mighty vessel.

"Wait for what?" he repeated.

"Viper Diamond Nine," Schiavo said, confirming my realization.

She'd brought Martin into her confidence regarding the power the President of the United States had granted her. The power to obliterate entire cities by ordering the launch of nuclear tipped missiles from a submarine that might, or might not, still be cruising the Pacific. I'd shared the same information with Elaine when Schiavo had given me that very same power. The two of us now held in our memory a series of letters and digits which would allow destruction to rain down upon a hostile town.

Or upon a lone aircraft carrier at sea.

"You're going to nuke the *Vinson*," Martin said.

"A hundred and thirty miles from Bandon," I said. "Is that a safe distance? There could be effects."

"It will be fine," she said.

"You sound confident," Martin said.

"I am."

Over the next few minutes she explained why what she was going to do would leave Bandon in the clear. But there was still one huge question to be answered.

"What if the sub isn't there anymore?" I asked and reminded her all at once.

"That's why Martin is here," Schiavo said, turning to her husband. "Fletch and I will put out the call to the sub. You get back to the plane and tell Beekman he's taking Westin, Hart, and Laws back to Bandon first. Before he heads back for us, I want him to have Lieutenant Lorenzen load three hundred pounds of C-Four on the plane."

I understood immediately.

"If the sub isn't out there, or can't hit the ship in time, we'll sink the *Vinson* ourselves."

Schiavo nodded at my supposition.

"We're on a clock, Martin," she said.

Her husband nodded, then left the bridge, limping as he made his way back to the flight deck. Schiavo looked to the radio in hand, coax cable running from its antenna port and disappearing beneath the open console.

"You remember the frequency, Fletch?"

I did, and I read it back to her from memory. She confirmed the numbers and entered them on the unit's keypad. She brought it up to her face and paused, looking at me for a moment before pressing the transmit button.

"This is Viper Diamond Nine," Schiavo said. "Please respond."

Schiavo released the mic switched and listened. There was only silence.

"This is Viper Diamond Nine," she repeated. "Come in."

Once more we listened, Schiavo dialing the radio's squelch down now to allow static through. If a weak signal was all the sub could manage, she didn't want it masked by the radio's noise cancelling feature.

"The three o'clock thing could be a hard rule," I said. "They may only surface at that time. If they're submerged, they're not going to hear a call from—"

"Viper Diamond Nine, this is the *USS Louisiana.*"

Schiavo looked to me, visibly shocked, as the reply cut me off.

"*USS Louisiana*," Schiavo said. "It's...good to...it's good to hear you're still with us."

There was a pause. A long pause. As if some discussion regarding our contact was happening on the receiving end. When the lack of response was becoming worrisome, the airwaves came to life again.

"This is the *USS Louisiana*," a different voice said. "Please identify."

It was an older voice. An authoritative voice. An impatient voice.

"This is Viper Diamond Nine," Schiavo said.

The next reply came back without any delay.

"Your name, Viper Diamond Nine."

Schiavo and I both puzzled at the question. There'd been no mention by the President that any authentication beyond the call sign would be required. But time had passed since that information was given to us. Years, actually. Those aboard the sub might not have had any contact with the nation's commander in chief, or any command authority, for a similar period. If so, any orders they'd been given might well have been superseded by the laws of necessity. And prudence.

"I say again, Viper Diamond Nine, I need your name."

I wasn't sure if the change in protocol had set something to simmer within, but the repeated insistence, in the mildest of ways, allowed what Schiavo was feeling to boil over.

"*USS Louisiana*, who am *I* speaking with?" Schiavo demanded.

A brief hesitation followed.

"This is the commanding officer," he replied.

"The protocol, you are aware, requires you to act on my request when received using the proper call sign," Schiavo reminded the man. "Am I incorrect?"

"You are not," the commanding officer said. "But those are three words, ma'am. I'm not blowing up some corner of the world based on three words I haven't heard since I was briefed on them several years ago."

Schiavo thought for a moment. The officer, whoever he was, had reverted to a level of command which forced more decisions upon himself. The rulebook which had run much of his operations had likely been used for toilet paper by now. He was having to improvise. Trust his gut. All from the claustrophobic isolation of a steel tube that spent most of its time cruising beneath the waves.

"What's your rank?" Schiavo asked, attempting to dial back the intensity of the impasse they'd reached.

"Captain," the man said, adding without prompting. "Captain Paul Vega."

Schiavo let a small breath slip out before keying the mic again.

"Paul, I'm Colonel Angela Schiavo, and I need something from you."

"Of course," Vega said, some surrender in his tone now. "What's your target, Viper Diamond Nine?"

"Not yet," Schiavo said. "I need your location."

"Colonel, that's information I wouldn't give God."

"I am not God, but I need to know if you are within three hundred miles of the Oregon coast."

"Colonel, as I said—"

"Captain Vega," Schiavo interrupted. "There are two reasons I need to know that information. The first relates to the target I am going to give you. The second relates to your resupply, which I'm assuming comes from the same place as ours—Hawaii."

Once more there was a contemplative lack of response. The man was weighing how much, considering the way the world was at this very moment, he could violate longstanding protocols.

"Captain Vega, there are no Russian subs stalking you," Schiavo told the reticent sub commander. "The reality is, you have a bigger problem."

"I haven't been able to reach Hawaii today," Vega said without further prodding. "After the jamming ceased, we tried, but every method which had been successful before only gave us dead air."

Now Schiavo had to be the bearer of news that was likely more horrible than a mere cutoff of supplies. The sub, which was miraculously still on station, was crewed by sailors. Sailors with families, almost certainly. And, to allow those sailors to function free of concern for their loved ones, it was logical to assume that the government had afforded them protection and provided for them in what was believed to be the safest of places.

Which, we now knew, turned out to not be that at all.

"Hawaii is gone, Captain Vega," Schiavo said, offering the sobering news without any attempt to sugarcoat it. "A captured cache of nuclear weapons was detonated there."

The silence that followed now lingered. The man on the other end of the transmission, and, possibly, those around him who'd heard what Schiavo had just shared, were reacting amongst themselves to this news. Debating its validity, I imagined. Discounting its source. None of that, though, would change the reality they, and we, now faced.

We were on our own. All we had to to taste that new normal was survive what Lana had planned for Bandon.

"Captain..."

"Yes," Vega replied, a change in his voice. "I'm here."

Between his words, in background chatter, other voices were parrying. Challenging the news. Supporting the possibility. It was a mutiny of acceptance.

"Those weapons were transported to Hawaii aboard the *USS Eisenhower*," Schiavo explained. "Another batch of those weapons are aboard the *USS Carl Vinson*. Captain, I'm standing on that ship right now."

"Excuse me..."

"Also aboard this ship is the person who put this all in motion," Schiavo said. "We're at anchor right now, but if she's true to her word, this vessel will sail toward our home, Bandon, and wipe out the survivor colony there in the same way Hawaii was obliterated."

"If this is true, why don't you stop her?" Vega challenged.

"Because we can't. She's sealed herself off with guards. We can't get to her. But you can."

Schiavo took just a minute to tell Vega what she wanted.

"Are you close enough to make this work?" Schiavo asked.

"Yes," Vega answered.

"You've got to hit this ship at the agreed upon time," Schiavo told him. "We have to have time to get off before she starts moving."

"Understood," Vega said, though he wasn't done. "Colonel Schiavo..."

"Yes?"

"You're certain about Hawaii?"

"Unfortunately, I am, Captain Vega. Prior to even learning of the action from the woman responsible, we detected an energy pulse from the area of the Pacific that correlates to Hawaii. This was noted even before we cut power to the jammer on this ship. Only a nuclear blast would produce enough to be heard over the interference."

"I see."

"I'm sorry," Schiavo said.

A final time there was an interlude of quiet. Ten seconds, maybe, where the naval officer finished weighing what he could do with what was needed.

"It will be the pleasure of the crew of the USS *Louisiana* to fulfill the mission you've given us, Colonel Schiavo."

"Thank you, Captain Vega," Schiavo said, an addendum coming to her before ending the communication. "You are welcome to sail to Bandon for supplies."

"Thank you," Vega said. "But once we complete your mission, we're going to Hawaii. To see for ourselves."

It wasn't doubt informing Vega's decision, I knew. It was necessity. If all there had been lost, his sailors deserved to see that with their own eyes.

"Godspeed," Schiavo said.

Noah Mann

"Thank you," Vega said. "And Colonel Schiavo, be off that carrier before we hit it. If you're not...then Godspeed to you."

The transmission ended. Schiavo handed the radio to me and looked out at the rain cascading past the bridge's windows.

"Try Bandon," Schiavo told me.

I entered the frequency we knew would be monitored and tried to make contact three times, without success.

"It's just too far," I said. "We don't have com gear in town like the *Louisiana* has."

Schiavo nodded. Any word to Bandon on what it might be facing would have to come from another source.

"Let's get that plane airborne," she said.

I lay the radio down atop the open console and followed her off the bridge.

Twenty Five

Hart, Laws, and Westin were aboard the Cessna, none without protesting the fact that they were leaving their commanding officer behind. But none would violate her orders, either. They would rather die than do that.

"Get on the radio when you're close enough and give Lieutenant Lorenzen a heads up so the C-Four is ready to load when you land," Schiavo said.

She stood next to the Cessna, talking to Beekman through the open door next to the pilot.

"You really think you can sink this ship with three hundred pounds of plastic explosives?" Beekman asked.

"I hope we don't have to find out," Schiavo said. "Get my guys home and get back here."

"What, you don't want to go down with the ship?" Beekman asked, shouting as he started the Cessna's engine.

"I'm not Navy!" Schiavo answered. "It would be bad form!"

Beekman gave her a quick smile, appreciating the quip she'd returned fire with. He closed his door and throttled up. He and Westin had already unhooked the plane from its tie-downs, the other members of the garrison joining to help turn the aircraft manually to line it up for a takeoff.

"Landing has to be harder than taking off," Martin said. "Right?"

"We'll know in a minute," I said.

The Cessna's engine revved as the brakes held it in place, the narrow bow of the carrier less than 500 feet away, that precipice nearly lost in the mix of weather and darkness. Only the cold waters of the Pacific lay beyond it should the aircraft not get airborne in time.

Then, the plane began to roll, accelerating, the deck pitching beneath it.

"He's not gonna make it," Martin said, stepping awkwardly away from the partial shelter of the island's exterior.

"Come on," I said, imploring the Cessna to fly. "Do it."

They were a hundred feet from the edge of the flight deck. Then fifty.

Forty.

Ten.

"Wheel's up," Schiavo said, just shy of an exclamation.

The Cessna's landing gear left the deck a scant few yards before that surface ended, the racing hum of its engine dissipating quickly as the aircraft disappeared into the night.

"Having Beekman load all that C-Four will slow down his return to get us," I said. "You sure you want to risk that after talking to the *Louisiana*?"

"What if they fail?" Schiavo suggested. "We won't be here to know."

I understood what she was planning.

"You want to set the charges no matter what," I said.

She nodded.

"We'll set them the best we can, as fast as we can down on the hangar deck, with a twenty-minute fuse," Schiavo said. "With any luck we'll open a gash on the side of the ship that will reach to the waterline."

"Let's hope Captain Vega makes all that unnecessary," I said.

"Absolutely," Schiavo agreed. "Now let's get out of this rain. We can cover the deck from the bridge."

She turned toward the entrance to the interior of the island, but Martin didn't. He stepped further out into the rain, limping across the deck toward the large cube which contained what had brought us here.

"Martin..."

He paused and looked back to his wife.

"We haven't seen what's inside," he said.

"There's no way in," I said.

Westin and Laws had scouted the perimeter of the object while on deck, they'd reported. It was sealed, only a small opening in place to allow the power cables to pass through.

"Martin, come give your leg a rest," Schiavo said.

Instead, he looked back to the object, the wall facing him twenty feet high. It was a smooth slab of some synthetic material, hard enough to keep anyone out, yet able to allow the jamming signal through without degrading it. In essence, the monolithic structure was a simple radome in place to protect, and conceal, the equipment within.

"You don't even want to see?" he asked. "You don't want to know?"

"No," Schiavo said, walking out to stand next to her husband.

I moved to join them, soaked already. The weather was working on us. Exhaustion, too. And pain. Martin, most of all, was facing the latter, his leg clearly hurting more than he was letting on. Worse, by far, than my finger. Still, he was ignoring it. Maybe, I thought, this mental excursion to what was hidden within the cube was partly an exercise in distraction.

"It doesn't matter," I said. "It won't exist in a little while."

He shook his head, at the cube, first, and then as he turned to eye the island, and the ship it rose from.

"We almost get done in by a bug that has it in for everything green, and then someone who's bothered by the fact that it didn't finish the job and take all of humanity with it turns to technology to finish us off. Some scientist creates the bug sixty years after other scientists make possible the bombs we're sitting on. Science created this ship. Its reactors. The thing inside that cube."

Martin paused his diatribe for a moment, growing still and contemplative before he looked to the flight deck and shook his head once more.

"Science couldn't save my son, but it can end the world," he said, looking up at his wife and me. "Where did this all start to go wrong?"

I'd known Martin Jay to be a strong man, with a passionate belief in his town, and in himself. He'd wielded so much power and influence through the darkest times, partly in hopes of keeping his ailing son alive. When Micah Jay succumbed to the medical issues which had plagued him, Martin had pressed on, leading the town which owed so much to him, and to his late son. I'd never witnessed him express confusion, nor bitterness, to the degree he now was.

"One person decides we all should die, and she can make that happen?" Martin asked, knowing that neither Schiavo or I would be able to soothe him with any definitive response. "Maybe we are the true blight."

"Some are," Schiavo said. "She is. And that sort of belief can spread, just like the grey grit moved from tree to bush to weed. Her thinking infected others."

Schiavo reached out and took hold of the M4 slung across her husband's chest.

"You can kill Fletch and me right now," she said. "With this. But you don't. Because it's not in your head, or your heart, to kill. You only do so when you're forced to, and you don't chalk it up to some forced ideology that says humanity was a mistake from the beginning."

She let go of his weapon and let it hang again from its sling.

"That woman," Schiavo continued, "the hate was in her heart before she had the means to act on it."

Martin absorbed what his wife had laid out to him. He glanced back to the large cube, then faced us again.

"I'm sorry," he said. "I don't let things... I mean, this is so beyond anything I've had to wrap my head around. I fought so hard to keep Micah alive. So many people did. And Lana, she has the power to negate anything good. I just don't..."

"No one does, Martin," I said, agreeing with the incomplete, but not unknown, sentiment. "How can you understand madness?"

"You think she's crazy?" Martin asked, probing my estimation of the woman he'd not been face to face with.

"No," I said. "I think she's evil."

The rain picked up, pushed by rising winds. Martin looked away from me, staring into the storm for a moment.

"Let's get out of this," Schiavo said. "Martin?"

He turned to her and nodded.

"Okay," he said.

We left the deck and headed into the island before making our way up to the bridge. I paused at the entrance, looking back to the flight deck and the maelstrom of weather pounding it. It was true that we were facing evil in human form, but we were also facing extreme circumstances and the tests that Mother Nature was throwing at us. For Schiavo, Martin, and me, the effects could be minimized by seeking the shelter that we were. But for Chris Beekman...

In a few hours, he would have to land once again on the pitching carrier in the stormy darkness. That wasn't any manifestation of evil, but it could kill him just as easily. And all of us in the process.

Part Four

Danger Close

Twenty Six

Two and a half hours after the Cessna rose from the deck with its four souls aboard, when Chris Beekman was almost certainly on his way back for his final taxi run of this mission, a series of explosions shook the *Vinson*. Four sharp blasts that ripped the nighttime stillness in quick succession, seeming to bracket the bow of the vessel.

"What was—"

"Shhh," Martin said, cutting me off.

I did as he said. So did his wife. The three of us tuning our ears through the remnants of the detonations to notice the unmistakable sound of big metal dragging across bigger metal.

"The anchor chains," Schiavo said.

We moved to the starboard side of the island and found a vantage point on an exterior platform hanging over the right side of the ship. Looking forward from that position we could, between flashes of lightning, see that the anchor chain on this side of the *Vinson* had been severed. Smoke drifting from where it had penetrated the hull indicated that some sort of shaped charges had cut the massive steel links, untethering the carrier from her anchors.

"That was coordinated," Martin said.

Schiavo nodded, but had something to add.

"More than that," she said. "It was planned. Long before we got here."

"Why set the ship adrift?" I wondered aloud. "The current here will push us southwest. It will end up nowhere near—"

The sudden jolt of motion ended the necessity that I finish my train of thought. We were moving. Slowly, but the giant ship was beginning to cut through the waves.

"Northwest," Martin said. "We're heading northwest."

"Right toward Bandon," Schiavo said.

I let out a grim chuckle, realizing too many things right then for any revelation to be welcome.

"That's why she didn't come after us," I said, the fact that had troubled me resurfacing. "It wasn't so she didn't waste more of her crew chasing us down. She doesn't need a crew. This was all planned to be automatic so no one can get cold feet."

"Lana isn't even necessary," Martin said, agreeing. "There's some computer deep inside the ship somewhere that's in control now. She could have blown her brains out already."

Schiavo thought on these new events, and likely explanations. One part, though, she did not agree with.

"She's still with us," she said. "She's not dead. Being here at that final moment is what holds meaning for her. Experiencing that last instant of life as it ends in a flash."

I nodded. The woman would not take her life as the others had. There would be no rope nor bullet for her.

"How fast are we moving?" I asked.

"I don't know," Martin said. "But these ships can get up to thirty knots."

"At that speed it'll be on top of Bandon in just over four hours," I said.

"We can't let it move," Schiavo said. "Forget home, for now. If it moves ten miles the strike we called in may never hit it."

I instinctively looked around the gutted bridge, hoping to spot something of use. Some cable to be cut. Anything. But there was nothing. All we had was us.

"We have to go back below," I said, looking to Martin. "You can cover the deck and stay off that leg."

Martin shifted weight onto his bad leg and grimaced through the pain. He brought his M4 up and clicked the selector to switch to burst mode.

"I'm not sitting this out," he said.

Schiavo waited just a moment, closing her eyes as she nodded.

"Maybe she still won't care," Schiavo said as she stood. "Maybe the way below will be clear."

"Maybe," Martin said, attempting to allow the possibility.

"None of us really believe that, right?" I said.

"Right," Schiavo said, bringing her shotgun up.

"Right," Martin agreed.

* * *

We jogged across the flight deck through waves of rain and wind threatening to push us off the rolling ship. Once more we slid down the rope to the hangar deck, its dimly lit expanse another point of vulnerability. Yet again, we crossed it, covering each other, making our way to the stairs, then transferring from balcony to balcony, until we were back in the part of the *Vinson* cut off from the rest.

Back in Lana's domain.

The machinery humming further below us sent soft, monotone vibrations through the ship. I could feel the propellers turning as the *Vinson* accelerated. It was an older ship, not as quiet as her newer brethren, I assumed. Silence didn't matter now, though. Pedal to the metal would be the order of the day in the operation Lana had conceived.

How many, though, had she coopted? This was not all her doing. At one time I would have considered it shocking that anyone would throw in with a person like her, and commit to helping bring about the end of our species. Especially those with the technical skills to help her make this happen. Engineers. Physicists. Tradesmen. People who bore those titles would have also had to subscribe to Lana's apocalyptic vision. Thinking minds, calculating intellects, gritty know-how, were all qualities of those who wanted to die along with the rest of humanity.

She'd made that happen. And I knew why Schiavo had stated what she had about Lana—the woman would never miss the end she'd envisioned. She was still here.

That meant we had to be on guard.

"How far down will we have to go?" Schiavo asked, looking to me.

I had an inkling why she had posed the question to me. I had built many things in my life, though nothing approaching the complexity of a nuclear-powered aircraft carrier. Still, there could be similarities in the concepts, and universal realities such as heat rising and cold air falling.

"You put the boiler in the basement," I said.

"I didn't get to the lower decks on Lana's part of the ship," Martin said. "She could have a menagerie down there for all we know."

I wouldn't be surprised at anything we might come across, but we absolutely had to locate whatever was controlling the ship and bring the vessel to a stop.

"All right," Schiavo said. "I'm on point."

Martin glanced to me. It was not her place to be at the front of a column, no matter how much she wanted to lead. But there was one major difference here which negated the concern we both were sharing—she had no troops to lead. Just us. Civilians.

"Okay," Martin said.

He had to accept her decision, as did I. There was no time to argue the point in any case. Every minute we delayed, the carrier sailed further away from the point Schiavo had called the strike in on, and closer to the people we cared about.

Schiavo moved out, leading us to our first set of stairs, the steep set of treads awkward to negotiate with weapons at the ready. There was no further way to descend where the stairs let out, just corridors straight ahead and to the left.

"We're going to have to cross over to—"

The lights went suddenly out, plunging us into darkness.

Twenty Seven

I moved toward a compartment opening I'd noticed, feeling
for the edge of the doorway that would lead into it.

"I'm covering left," Schiavo said.

But left of what? Her left? Mine? In the inky world into
which we'd been plunged, we could be aiming at each other
and not even realize it.

"There's a space here," I said.

Everything was by feel. Schiavo and I had had our gear,
including flashlights, confiscated by Lana's people.

But Martin hadn't been with us. He still retained all his
gear, including the weapon light on his M4, a fact Schiavo
realized at the same instant I did.

"Martin, give us some light," she said.

There was a brief hesitation before he responded.

"I can't," he said.

His reply was too calm. Too monotone. Something was
wrong, and a second later, both Schiavo and I knew the
precise nature of the problem.

"Go ahead," Lana said. "Turn it on."

My finger slid onto the Benelli's trigger just before a
wash of brightness filled the narrow corridor, the beam of
Martin's weapon light splashing off the floor to reveal not
only Schiavo and I crouched against opposite walls, but also
Martin several feet away, Lana standing behind him, the
barrel of a sawed-off Remington pump pressed against my
friend's back. Her face was partly obscured by a set of night

vision goggles, infrared emitter atop them allowing her to see in complete darkness.

"Guns on the floor," she said, flipping the goggles upward to see us with unaided vision.

We did as she instructed, Martin, too, his light now spread along the length of the corridor.

"Where are all your masked men?" I challenged her.

She brought a boot up and planted it on Martin's back, shoving him toward us with a kick. He recovered and turned to face our captor.

"Do you believe I need them?" Lana asked. "Circumstances would seem to indicate I'm doing quite well on my own."

"Can you stop the ship?" Schiavo asked, leaping to a direct inquiry that actually seemed to surprise the woman.

"No," Lana said. "But I can stop you."

She took a step backward, giving herself a few feet more distance to us. To her targets. We could rush her, and if she began firing there was no doubt in my mind that we would fight. But, even as she'd backed away, she did not begin to fire.

"I remember something," she said. "I think of it often. It was when I was a child in Poland. A very young child. Not even in school yet."

For some reason she'd drifted off into a monologue. As long as she was talking, she wasn't shooting. But every second that she kept us here, at bay, the *Vinson* moved closer and closer to Bandon, and away from the location that Schiavo had given to the *Louisiana*.

"We had a dog," Lana continued, the shotgun shifting every few words so that its aim landed on each of us. "A stray. My mother said we had nothing to feed the dog. But I saved scraps from the table and fed it when I would go outside to play. One day, my mother caught me doing this, and she disciplined me. She told me there was not enough food for the dog. So I had to stop feeding it."

Sounds echoed through the ship, sharp and quick. Lana hesitated, listening, discounting the errant noises which were likely products of cut beams reacting to motion through the violent sea.

"Then, the dog had puppies. She gave birth behind a shed in a pile of rotting hay. For days she tried to feed them, but she had no food for herself. I begged my mother to let me feed the mother dog, but she beat me for asking."

Lana quieted for a moment, a weird, teary smile curling her lips as the childhood memory mixed with some twisted adult disdain.

"One puppy died every day for a week, until they were all gone. Then the mother died a few days later. Animals dragged away the bodies and devoured them. But that is what animals do."

She shifted the aim very deliberately toward Schiavo now.

"My mother had hair like you," Lana said.

"Is this supposed to explain why you're doing what you're doing?" Martin asked. "Because you had a heartless mother?"

"There are too many heartless mothers," Lana said. "And fathers. And people in general. We've all done enough damage, to each other, to the planet."

"Killing us, killing everyone, won't erase what happened to those puppies," I said.

She shook her head slightly at me.

"I've seen worse than dead puppies in my life," Lana sneered. "*That* is what this is about. The carnage, the indifference, that man is capable of. It needs to stop."

Her shotgun shifted to me.

"It has to stop now," she said.

Her finger lay very plainly on the trigger. I sensed Schiavo and Martin both tense off to my side. It was about to happen. Some of us, hopefully, would survive.

Even then, with our failure in this attempt to stop the ship, death would catch up soon enough.

BOOM!

It wasn't an explosion, but it sounded like one, the crack of the shotgun amplified in the confines of the corridor. A flash, too, erupted as the weapon was fired.

But neither came from Lana's sawed-off Remington.

Her body jerked forward, gun falling from her grip, a splatter of blood showering the wall next to her as her body bounced off of it and folded in half, slamming hard onto the floor. Behind her, in the silhouetted shadows cast by Martin's light, Chris Beekman stood, his own shotgun smoking in his hands. He racked a fresh round into the chamber and covered the woman he'd just taken out without a second to spare.

"Chris," I said, grabbing my Benelli and rising. "How did..."

"Number one, tail wind," he said.

On the floor, Lana gurgled, blood spilling from her mouth, her breath bubbling as she choked within.

"Number two, Sergeant Hart likes to talk," Beekman said. "He described how you all made it back topside. I just reversed the order when I couldn't find you on the flight deck. Then I followed that nutjob's voice."

I silently thanked the garrison's medic for his chatty nature and his mind mapping abilities. Schiavo stood and kicked Lana's shotgun away, picking up her own Benelli as Martin grabbed his M4 from the floor.

"Did you bring the C-Four?" Schiavo asked.

"Plenty," Beekman told her.

The arrival of the explosives had changed the equation for Schiavo, and negated the necessity of our mission into the depths of the ship to find what was controlling it.

"All right," Schiavo said. "We're heading back up. We'll take the time to transfer the charges down to this level and place them all along the starboard side of the ship. I can't imagine that three hundred pounds of C-Four wouldn't punch a hole in—"

She stopped, her gaze angling toward the very side of the ship she'd been referencing. The starboard side. Martin, too, looked, directing his M4 there, though not at any overt threat, but to wield his light and illuminate the corridor where our attention had refocused.

"Dear God," Schiavo said.

The same dread that sparked her reaction flared suddenly in me. In all of us.

"What the hell is that?" Beekman asked, the sound rising now, echoing through the *Vinson*'s hull.

"Torpedoes," Martin said.

Twenty Eight

We heard it just seconds before it hit, the sound of the whirring propellers transmitted through the carrier's steel hull in the same way that a pinging sonar must have terrified World War Two submariners. There'd been no expectation when Schiavo had ordered the strike that we'd still be aboard when it hit. Though less lethal than one of the nukes the boomer could have unleashed, what the colonel had ordered would leave no chance of radioactive fallout that could affect Bandon.

Torpedoes...

It had been her idea, and her call, to utilize the sub's other choice of weaponry. An inspired choice, I'd thought then. Now, it seemed *we* would be taken out by the underwater ordnance, not just the carrier.

"Run," Martin said, in as calm a voice as I'd ever heard him use.

Beekman turned first, but only made it a few steps before we heard two distinct sources of the sound seem to dive beneath us, to a position directly below the keel of the carrier.

Then they exploded.

Martin's weapon light stayed on, and, strangely, the emergency lights which previously had glowed dim throughout the vessel flickered back to life as the blast tore through the decks below us. I was hurled upward, into the corridor's ceiling, as were my friends.

Except Schiavo.

The wall next to her bent in her direction, and the floor split along a twenty-foot length, directly beneath her feet. The fissure spread open like a steely, screaming maw, swallowing Lana, her body disappearing in a sudden gush of misty spray.

"Angela!"

It was Martin, horrified, calling out to his wife as he recovered from the impact. I looked and saw what was terrifying him.

The same jagged hole, which had taken Lana whole, also had Schiavo, only her upper half visible, everything from the waist down pinned in the torn steel.

"Help me!" Martin said.

He scrambled to his wife over the buckled floor, Beekman and I joining him. Schiavo looked to us, her gaze clear, both hands planted on exposed supports pressed against her hips, pushing for all she was worth.

"Are you hurt?" Martin asked, setting his M4 aside and giving her a quick look.

"I don't...think so," Schiavo said.

Beekman took a flashlight from his pocket and shined it all over Schiavo.

"I don't see any blood," the pilot said.

"Let's pull you out of there," I said.

Martin and I each grabbed her under the arms and pulled.

"AHHH!" Schiavo shouted. "Stop!"

We eased our grip on her.

"What is it?" Martin asked, kneeling next to his wife.

Schiavo tried to shift her body, turning against the metal to no avail.

"There's something sharp pressing on my hip, and my legs are bent against a pipe. Or a bunch of pipes."

I grabbed the flashlight from Beekman and bent close to the narrow hole, peering into the gap just next to Schiavo. What I saw made my heart sink, and my soul hurt.

The entire structure beneath us had been sheared in half, and Schiavo was in between, the two parts having sprung back together after the blast. Only a small deformation in one steel beam had allowed her to not be cut in half, pinning her instead.

"How is it, Fletch?" Martin asked.

I looked up to Schiavo.

"Can you turn at all?" I asked. "Just to get one hip past that beam?"

She tried again, cranking her upper body, hoping that would make the lower half follow. But it didn't. She stopped, spent from the effort, and looked to me.

"I can't," she said.

Martin lay flat on the floor and grabbed at the inch-thick steel that had been ripped and peeled in the blast. He pulled, and pulled, his effort magnificent and futile and heartbreaking all at once. After a moment Schiavo reached out and put a hand gently on his shoulder.

"Stop, Martin."

He did, his gaze meeting hers, one desperate, and the other resigned to what had been made inevitable.

"Immovable object," she said. "It's no use."

Martin drew a few breaths, surveying the carnage once more.

"Are you sure?" he asked his wife. "Are you really sure?"

She nodded.

"If it was just my leg, I'd say cut it off. But it's not just my leg."

She was accepting her fate, and trying to convince her husband to do the same. I wasn't ready to give in yet, though. Once more I looked into the fissure, reaching down, searching for some piece of steel that might just be hanging on by a thread. If I could get a solid grip and move it just a few inches...

"Fletch..."

I pulled back from the hole and looked to her.

"Get out of here," Schiavo said, shifting her attention to her husband. "You, too."

Martin smiled and shook his head.

"Nice try," he said.

Schiavo twisted her upper body against the force pinning her below the waist, seeking more comfort than release. She'd already come to accept that there was no escaping the hold the mangled steel had on her.

"You don't have much time," Schiavo said, looking between Martin and me. "The ship is going down."

Around us all, the ship groaned and screamed, metal twisting against the assault of the sea pouring in several decks below us, the *Vinson* reacting to the flooding as any ship would.

"The ship is starting to list," Beekman said.

"You don't have time to pretend you can save me," Schiavo told Martin. "Chris won't be able to take off if the deck reaches too steep an angle."

I looked to the pilot. He said nothing. No words to dispute or agree with Schiavo's estimation. Which meant she was right.

"I'm not pretending anything," Martin said.

He sat next to his wife on the buckled floor. From below, icy air was gushing through ruptures in the structure as the rapid inflow of seawater displaced the atmosphere trapped in the lower decks. It was as if some chilled, bitter wind was adding its concurrence to Schiavo's acceptance of her fate. This had become a place of death, and it would take more lives still.

"You can't do this," Schiavo pleaded with her husband.

Martin took her hand in his and looked to Beekman and me. He was frantic no more. If anything, for himself and for his wife, he was at peace.

"You both need to get moving," he said.

I looked at Martin, and then Schiavo. Her husband's words, and his own acceptance of what was to come, had eased her insistence that he leave her behind. In its place there rose a calmness, one tinged by sadness that, of all places, this would be the end of them.

But not all of us.

"Fletch, you have to go," Schiavo said, echoing Martin's words. "Consider it an order, if that's necessary."

"I'm a civilian," I said, not wanting to fully accept the inevitable.

"Then go because you have a wife, and a child, who both need you," Schiavo said. "Isn't that reason enough?"

It was. And she knew it.

"Fletch," Beekman said. "She's right about the deck. We don't have much time."

The decision was made, if not in my heart, then in my head. I would never be okay with what I was about to do, but leaving them, leaving my friends behind, was the only thing I could do.

"The best worst option," I said, echoing something we'd faced earlier.

"It is," Schiavo said.

As if to emphasize the gravity of the moment, of the decision, the *Vinson* rattled severely, mimicking the power of an earthquake within. The great vessel was in her death throes.

"Fletch..."

I nodded at Beekman's urging.

"I'm going to miss you both," I said.

Martin nodded and turned to face his wife. Schiavo, a skim of tears glazing her eyes, smiled and spoke her final words to me.

"Go, Fletch."

* * *

Chris Beekman and I retraced our path back to the flight deck, moving through twisted corridors and crossing the same precarious pair of balconies. We crossed the hangar deck and shimmied up the rope a final time, jogging past the quieted jamming transmitter before climbing into the Cessna, its fuselage matching the list to starboard, the angle growing more severe with every passing minute. The *Vinson*, still under power, had seen its intended course upset by the impact of the torpedoes. The growing weight of water filling its hull was pulling the mighty ship into a wide turn to the right. It would never reach Bandon.

We might not, either.

"This is gonna be tricky," Beekman said once he was belted in, his headset on. "If that's even the right word. Insane also comes to mind."

"You can do this at this angle?"

He started the aircraft's engine, the propeller spinning up past the rain-splattered windshield.

"If I can't, at least we'll make a nice boom on impact with the water," he said, tipping his head toward the back seat.

I looked and saw what he was referencing. In the excitement below, I'd forgotten that he'd loaded the plane with C4. From the looks of it, the 300 pounds Schiavo requested had been fulfilled, and then some. There was enough explosive material onboard now to—

The thought, the possibility, hit me in a flash, memory and plan coalescing in that instant.

"Stop," I said, as Beekman was about to advance the throttles.

"What is it?"

I took my headset off and unbuckled my safety belt, then pushed the passenger door open and stepped out onto the flight deck.

"Fletch!" Beekman shouted, stripping his own headset off. "What the hell are you doing?"

I tipped the passenger seat forward and grabbed four individual C4 charges, two pounds each, with detonator and blasting caps already stuffed in a small gear bag.

"How long can you wait?" I asked Beekman.

"Fletch, you—"

There was no time to entertain any protests he had in mind. I needed an answer to quickly gauge the usefulness of what I was thinking.

"Give me an honest answer. Best guess. Whatever you have."

Beekman gaped at me, processing the almost impossible question. Weighing the deteriorating condition of the ship, the weather, and the capabilities of the plane. And of himself.

"Ten minutes," he said. "But what are you going to do?"

I shoved the C4 in the gear bag and slung the collection of demolition materials over my shoulder.

"If we're not back by then, take off," I told him.

"Fletch, what the hell are you going to do?"

I didn't even know how to describe it in a way that wouldn't take minutes. Minutes that I didn't have. There *was* a way to lay it out to him, though. A way more rooted in truth that any technical explanation would be.

"The impossible," I said.

Twenty Nine

Once more, for the final time, I hoped, I descended into the bowels of the dying ship. The emergency lights were humming and crackling, on the verge of failing completely, and every wave which slammed into the leaning ship as it turned felt like it was going to push it fully over onto its side.

But they didn't. Through the strobing lights and a mist developing within the ship's passageways, I pressed forward, and downward, reaching the spot where Schiavo and Martin held each other, the sound of rushing water plain just two decks below them.

"Fletch," Schiavo said, upon seeing me. "There's nothing you can—"

I held the bag of demolition gear out to her and handed Martin my shotgun.

"There's something I can try," I said. "Look, all we need to do is loosen the floor structure below you. If that shifts eight inches, six inches, you'll be freed."

"You want to blow the structure beneath us?" Martin asked, not quite shocked by what I was proposing.

"Down one deck and thirty feet to port," I said.

"And that eight-inch movement could just as easily be in the other direction," Martin reminded me. "That would kill her."

I had to accept his premise, but I had to believe that there was a chance it would work. Maybe one in ten. But it was her only chance to escape being entombed in a watery grave.

"Your call, Angela," I said.

She looked to the battered floor, and to the hole she'd been pulled into. The mix of overpressure from the rushing air and the moisture within the vessel had let a fog build, obscuring much of what lay just a few yards away. But she could feel what was coming. She could sense, and hear, the water rising below. She would either drown when it rose to this deck, or when the *Vinson* finally capsized and slipped beneath the sea.

"Angela," I began, prompting her to make a decision quickly. "I survived that blast in the pit up in Skagway. You all dug me out of that. I'm not going to stand by and let you die if there's a chance I can return the favor and get you out of here."

She looked quickly to Martin. He was either going to watch her die in a hail of fire and twisting steel, or when water filled her lungs. Or, he could have some hope that the best worst option this time would work in our favor.

He nodded and Schiavo looked to me.

"Do it," she said.

"I've got a one-minute fuse," I said, grabbing my shotgun from Martin. "When I fire, that's the countdown beginning."

I stood and, without any further exchange, raced off down the hazy passageway.

* * *

The deck below was a disaster zone when I reached it. Through a web of broken, jagged metal, where floor and walls had been peeled apart, I could just see the bottom of Schiavo's boots. Her legs rested upon a length of piping that had been almost knotted by the impact of the torpedoes. This, I knew, was my mark. I had to set the charges a dozen yards past where I stood. There, they would blow and relieve the strain which had buckled the lower decks upward, pinning my friend in the hole that opened beneath her.

That was the plan.

I pushed forward through the mist, acrid hints of fluids from burst pipes thick in the air. In places, water already sloshed around my boots where the floor sank and rose. Everything around me informed my realization that, despite any drawbacks, haste was the order of the moment.

The ship could sink. Another shift could crush Schiavo. Beekman might not be able to take off.

Time...

I had to hurry. For her sake. For everyone's. I wanted to see my family again, as much as I wanted to save my friend. There was no time I could afford to waste.

Obstacles before me I simply ignored, crossing them or, if possible, heaving them aside. When I'd moved the correct distance from Angela's location I began setting the charges, placing the four packages in a line that stretched from the corridor into an adjacent compartment. I connected them together, inserting the blasting caps, each silvery plug slipping into the plasticky material. The end of the fuse that ran from charge to charge was topped by a simple plunge detonator. Once I pushed it down, I would have one minute to return to my friends.

One minute...

I aimed the Benelli into a side corridor and fired. The crack of the shot echoed sharp as the double ought pellets ricocheted off into the distance. My thumb depressed the synthetic plunger and a soft hiss sounded as the fuse was lit, a bright flame sizzling slowly along its length toward the charges.

Go...

I retraced my steps, climbing over debris, the water near my knees now in places. All I had to do was make it through the opening at the end of the passageway and up a steep set of stairs, and I would be back with Schiavo and Martin, ready to hold onto her as the blast was set off.

That never happened.

The *Vinson* did not cooperate, a shift in the massive ship causing the fractured floor beneath me to drop just shy of the stairs. My feet slipped out from under me, the shotgun tumbling from my grip and sinking as I plunged into black water.

Thirty seconds...

That was how long remained, I estimated, before the eight pounds of C4 detonated. If I remained where I'd fallen, submerged in the space below, all the structure above which I'd wanted to free would come crashing down, trapping me, if not killing me outright.

"Fletch..."

I heard a faint call. It was Martin's voice, obviously wondering where I was after signaling that the fuse had been lit. He'd obviously heard and felt the further collapse of the space below, but he could do nothing for me. He had to stay with his wife and keep her from falling once the charges freed the section of floor pinning her.

I was on my own.

The power of the rising water surprised me, but only until I realized that the full power of the ocean was pressing on the hull, and forcing seawater through the breech at tremendous pressure. It pushed me against submerged pieces of the broken structure, sharp metal jabbing my sides, My legs. My arms.

Twenty seconds...

Those sharp lengths of steel clawed at me as the water threw me against them. Quickly, though, I realized they might be the very things that saved me.

I planted one boot on the lowest one and stepped on it, lifting my body partly out of the water. Then I stepped onto the next one, using each like rungs on a ladder. Quickly I

was able to reach a section of the floor above and both pull
and push myself toward it, climbing free of the water.

Ten seconds...

I grabbed a length of exposed pipe as I swung a leg
onto the floor and rolled onto the open section, just ten feet
from the stairs.

Five seconds...

With only seconds left until the blast, I knew it was
going to be close. But not as close as it turned out to be.

Thirty

Five steps shy of the top of the stairs, the C4 went off. I felt the treads drop beneath me, the whole space seeming to shift away from the explosion. The mist which had formed within the ship was blown clear by the rush of hot gasses expanding from the point of detonation. I rolled away from the violent force, then righted myself and scrambled up the remaining steps on all fours.

"Fletch!"

Martin, again, was calling out to me, though now he sounded almost frantic. I left the stairs behind and ran the short distance to where I'd left them, where I found him holding his wife by the hands as the rest of her dangled over a watery abyss.

"Help!"

I did as he asked, and needed, taking one of Schiavo's hands from him and pulling as I planted a foot against the weakened wall for leverage. The charges had done just what I'd hoped, collapsing the structure beneath away from her. She swung her freed legs, searching for a foothold as Martin and I hauled her upward.

"We've got you," I said.

In the next few seconds we had her back on, relatively, solid ground.

"I'll hug you both later," she said, instinctively reaching for her weapon, but it was gone.

"Nothing left to shoot at," I said. "Let's go."

Martin was the only one of us still armed, his M4 lay snugly slung across his chest as we raced through the ship, up stairs, back across the balconies, which now tipped frighteningly close to the cresting waves below.

"This list is bad," Martin said as we reached the hangar deck.

"He can do it," Schiavo said.

I, too, had faith in Chris Beekman. But the reality was, I had no idea if he was still up there, on the flight deck. I'd been gone more than ten minutes. If he'd taken my word as an order to be followed at all costs, the three of us were going to go down with the *Vinson*.

Schiavo was first up the rope. I went next. Martin tied the end of the rope around his waist and we pulled him up, his injured leg swinging away from the edge of the elevator well as he swung back and forth. In less than a minute we had him topside.

Then, as best we could, we ran toward the jamming apparatus, nearing the edge of the cube where we would be able to see if the Cessna was still there. Before we ever reached that point, though, we knew.

Chris Beekman crossed in front of us, carrying an armful of C4 to the edge of the ship, where he tossed it into the sea. He saw us coming and waved at us to hurry.

"I cleared out the charges," he said.

The back seat was clear now. Schiavo and Martin climbed in. I took the front seat as Beekman sat behind the controls and started the engine once again. As he did, the Cessna began to slide, skidding a few inches at a time in the direction of the list, the damp deck only aiding the slippage.

"Hang on," Beekman said. "We've only got one shot at this."

He held the brake and revved the engine, the throttles firewalled. The plane shook around us, horsepower building, the propeller a deadly blur before us. He wanted to rocket away from a standstill, not slowly accelerate, something he'd done already.

But the ship was on an even keel on his previous takeoff. And the weather had not deteriorated to intermittent squalls, which were dragging curtains of rain across the flight deck, moving from port to starboard. This, I knew, as did Beekman, was going to be a takeoff to remember.

If it worked.

"Hang on," he said, and released the brake.

The Cessna lurched forward, toward the stern, drifting left with the list. Beekman compensated with rudder, building speed, the end of the truncated runway coming up fast.

"If anybody prays, now would be a good time," Beekman told us.

But there was no time to utter even a request to the Almighty, as the stern of the ship ended just beyond a sheet of rain, black ocean and snarling whitecaps past the windshield. Beekman eased the yoke back, bringing the nose up and leveling off into a shallow left turn.

"We're up," he said.

I looked back to my friends and saw Schiavo laying across Martin, holding him, neither bothering with seatbelts. The moment was too raw. Too real. They simply needed to embrace each other.

"That was incredible," I said, looking to Beekman.

He stayed focused ahead, but I saw him nod slightly at the compliment which he'd heard through the headset.

"Dave Arndt said I should take flying lessons," I told Beekman.

"He's a good pilot," Beekman said. "Had a sketchy instructor."

"All the same, I can't imagine doing what you just did."

"A couple days ago, Fletch, neither could I."

We continued to gain altitude until we were a few hundred feet over the dying ship, ambient moonlight filtering through the storm allowing enough definition to see that the *Vinson* was in its final minutes.

"She's down by the bow now," Martin said.

She was rolling onto her right side, with the front of the ship beginning to slip under the waves. We stayed in a low orbit over the *Vinson* as more and more of her settled beneath the roiling sea.

"There she goes," Beekman said.

In an almost graceful manner, the leviathan rolled fully over and dove, bow first, at a gentle angle, into the Pacific.

"What if the nukes go off?" Beekman asked as we watched the frothing spot on the water where the *Vinson* had just been. "Can they still explode down there?"

"Under seven thousand feet of water," Schiavo said. "We may never know."

Could the bombs still detonate if submerged? If they did, would they all work? And, if so, would the sea mitigate any effects. Visions of some tsunami triggered by a nuke briefly occupied my thoughts, but there was a lot of water to absorb and dissipate such a thing, I thought. Still, I would sleep better when days had passed with no indication that we were still facing some threat.

"How long until we're home, Chris?" Schiavo asked.

"Ninety minutes in this weather," he said, leaving the orbit and turning us toward shore.

"Okay," Schiavo said, letting herself rest against Martin's chest again as she closed her eyes. "Okay."

She was exhausted. Martin, too. Beekman had to be.

I was not.

We'd all been through so much. Martin had been hurt. Schiavo was banged up. Bruises and cuts dotted my body. A finger was broken. For some reason, though, my mind was alive. Sharp. Thinking.

People had given up, to be certain. In many places across the globe they had simply laid down and accepted their fate. Starvation, in most cases. Fewer had chosen Lana's path. One of an aggrandized self-loathing. Playing the blame game on humanity. We were bad. Evil. An evolutionary mistake unworthy of the planet which had harbored and sheltered and nourished us.

I didn't buy that one iota.

Something about the very act of despising others, members of the human race, to the point of designing an end to everything, gnawed at me. Judge *me*, not the me whose perception is based upon your experience with others. Hate the act, or the perpetrator, but not those who tread the same ground. Sitting at the same table as Lana, facing her, feeling her elevated disdain, I knew that she was incapable of such selective discrimination. Long ago, for her own twisted reasons, she'd decided that all were guilty.

Even herself.

We had enough to deal with without needing to concern ourselves with lunatics such as her who would wipe us out given the chance. That only reinforced my belief that Bandon had to evolve. It had to change. No longer was it the place where we were safest.

Somewhere was, though. Many somewheres were. We just had to find them.

Thirty One

We returned in as anticlimactic a manner as imaginable. The airwaves clear, Beekman reported that we were inbound. Despite the hour, just after dawn, it was Krista who received the radio call, relaying wind and precipitation readings from the town's weather station. The Cessna lined up on the runway from the south and settled onto the rainy runway with hardly a jolt to signal our return to terra firma.

We did not arrive to an empty field, however.

A Humvee and a pickup truck sat near the hangar, engines idling and their lights on in the stormy morning light. It was my pickup, I saw when Chris Beekman turned us off the runway. *Our* pickup.

The passenger door swung open as the plane stopped and I saw the wheelchair whip forward from the bed of the truck. A few seconds later Elaine was in it, wheeling her way toward the aircraft, the falling rain be damned. I climbed out and jogged toward her, meeting her well past the end of the wingtip. I bent and she pulled me into a hug, then kissed me.

"You're not hurt," she said, both asking and commenting as she eased back from our embrace.

"I'm fine," I said. "Knocked around a bit."

I'd tell her about the multiple explosions that had nearly killed me aboard the carrier later. Maybe.

Just beyond the plane, Schiavo was helping Martin toward the Humvee, Lt. Lorenzen leaving the driver's seat to assist her. In a minute they had him in the back seat.

Before Schiavo joined him, she looked my way, eyeing me through the rain, the headlight beams raising sparkles off each falling drop. She smiled, a real smile. Not just one of relief, though that was an obvious reaction she would be experiencing. This was something more. Something deeper. An appreciation that we had come through yet another challenge. Together.

Then, she brought her left hand up and tapped the ring finger.

My finger...

I'd completely forgotten about the injury I'd suffered when first rappelling down to the hangar deck. The digit had been broken, and the bandage job that Schiavo had done on it, unsurprisingly, was still intact. It was soaked, and a bit battered, but it had kept the injury from getting worse.

Of course, now that it had been brought to my attention, it began to throb like an elephant was standing on it.

Without a word or further gesture, Schiavo joined her husband in the Humvee. Elaine and I watched them drive off, and it was at that moment that an innocuous oddity struck me.

"By the way," I said, retrieving my mangled wedding ring from one of the cargo pockets in my pants. "We're going to have to replace this."

Elaine eyed the cut band, taking it from me, then noticed my bandaged finger for the first time.

"I thought you weren't hurt," she said, mildly scolding me.

"It's a finger," I said. "Hardly worth mentioning."

She regarded me with some mild annoyance, but let it go, dropping the ring in her shirt pocket.

"Who drove you here?"

"Molly," Elaine answered.

Molly Anne Beck, Private, United States Army, was one of Schiavo's newest recruits, nineteen years old, whip smart and tough as the day was long.

"That was nice of her to chauffer you," I said. "We can drop her off when we pick up Hope."

"We don't have to pick Hope up," Elaine said, then turned her wheelchair and rolled back toward the pickup's open door.

I followed, stopping in the light rain to peer inside, dome light revealing our little girl snuggled up against Molly, dead asleep next to the driver. I'd assumed that Grace was watching our daughter while Elaine came to meet me, but, instead, our child had woven her way into another's heart.

"She's an angel," Molly said, smiling.

"She can be," I said, hinting at the reality of parenting a two-year-old. "Slide over, I'll drive."

Elaine climbed in, soaking wet, as was I, but neither of us cared. I stowed her wheelchair in the bed of the pickup and went around to the driver's door as the trio of ladies, young and old, squished to one side.

"Fletch..."

I stopped with my hand on the driver's door and turned to see Chris Beekman standing there, as drenched as I was. He had an odd little smile on his face. Odd for him, I thought, as he was one who rarely expressed any hint of joy openly. He was a hard man. A solitary soul, most of the time.

"We're both going to catch pneumonia," I told him.

"Ironic if that's what finally lays us out," he said.

There was a moment of silence then. That awkward pause when nothing is said because there is too much to say.

"I'm an ass sometimes," Beekman said. "Full of myself. I know that."

"Everyone knows that, Chris," I added with a smile.

But he was serious. Some sort of self-reflection had set itself to spinning in his thoughts, and he was trying to express things that were difficult.

"I thought I was going to die, Fletch."

I looked at him and the smile was gone. Fear and wonder had replaced it in his eyes.

"When I came back to the carrier, and landed the second time, I had to approach from the stern because the wind had shifted."

For some reason, likely the hectic nature of our departure, I hadn't noticed that, in contrast to our initial arrival on the *Vinson*, which had been a straight in landing down the bow, our final departure from the sinking vessel had been facing the aft end of the carrier.

"It was dark," Beekman, said as we stood in the rain. "No lights on the carrier like when I took off. And the squalls were just, intense. I couldn't even see the deck until the last seconds."

Schiavo, Martin, and I hadn't witnessed what Beekman was describing. We were already below deck, searching for some way to stop the vessel from moving.

"You did an amazing job, Chris," I told him.

But to that he shook his head.

"It was luck," he said. "Nothing but luck on that last landing. There was no way I should have been able to put the plane down in one piece. None. Zero. My skillset was so far from what was required that it's laughable."

"But still you made it happen."

"I'm one percent of the reason it worked," he countered. "What I'm trying to say is...I think...I think this was all meant to be. I'm not some sappy guy who believes in destiny, but..."

He couldn't finish. He'd been overwhelmed by the events, and his part in them.

"Chris," I began, "sometimes luck is enough. But it's never enough unless someone's there to give it a chance to happen. That's what we all did. And at the end of the day, I'll take all the luck there is if it brings me home."

Beekman thought on that for a moment, then nodded. He reached out, offering his hand. I shook it as the rain began to pound, the storm building.

"Thank you," Beekman said.

He stepped back and raised a hand, giving a small wave to Elaine and Molly in the truck. Then he left us and made his way off toward the hangar. I let the rain wash over me for a moment, then I slid behind the wheel of the pickup.

"That didn't look like Beekman was being very Beekman," Elaine said past our sleeping daughter and Molly.

"He wasn't," I said.

Elaine nodded. She understood. She and I, and Martin, and Schiavo, and dozens more in our town, had faced death. Real, true, inevitable death, only to see the light of day again. There was no clear sunrise to greet Chris Beekman. That would come another day, when skies were clear. But he had most certainly faced his own moment of demise and come through it. He was changed.

We all were.

Thirty Two

I put the idling pickup into drive and made a wide turn around the parked Cessna, steering us to the airport driveway. A minute later we were on the road. In five we'd dropped Molly at the garrison headquarters where she was scheduled to 'stand watch' until noon, which would entail calling on Lt. Lorenzen should any situation develop that she couldn't handle.

"So?"

I looked to Elaine. She'd shifted our daughter onto a blanket to protect her from the water we were both shedding.

"So..." I repeated, prodding her to be more specific.

"You still feel the same after what you just did?" she asked.

On our flight back to town, after a few moments decompressing, Schiavo had gotten on the radio to brief her second in command on what had transpired. He had shared the information with Elaine, Bandon's mayor, as a matter of necessity. She was, in our little corner of the world, the highest elected authority we had access to. And she was pressing me on the fears I'd shared, and the way past those fears I'd outlined.

"More than ever," I said.

She was not surprised by my confidence. She was also not unaware of what it pointed to. If acted upon, all that we'd come to know, and to depend upon, would change. In irreversible ways.

"Wagon train," Elaine said as I drove.

"Come again?"

She cradled our bundled daughter and stared out the window, seized by some thought.

"It's really no different than pioneers setting out in wagons for new lands," my wife said. "We're just the new pioneers."

It was an apt comparison, with some small caveats. We'd be reclaiming land, and homes, from those who'd been lost to the blight and its aftermath. The landscape would not be unknown. And, hopefully, we'd not find ourselves in conflict with a native population.

Even with any hindrances and potential dangers, I knew we had to enter this new phase of survival. If we did not, another carrier, or another rogue army, or a government gone crazed with power, could finish us off. One and all.

We'd come too far to risk that.

* * *

We returned home and put our daughter to bed.

"You need sleep," Elaine said as she sat on our bed, pulling a fresh sweatshirt over her head after drying off.

I'd toweled down and changed, too. But with the sun rising beyond the storm, I felt nothing approaching tiredness. Physical exhaustion was plain in every muscle, and in the crispness of my thoughts. Still, for some reason, I did not want to lie down. Did not want to let dreams take me yet.

"You catch a few hours," I told Elaine. "Hope's going to be up in like an hour, so I'll deal with that. You can spell me later."

Elaine knew that I was not simply making an altruistic offer so she could sleep. She also knew me well enough to realize that some things I had to work out for myself.

"Okay," she said.

She reached down and moved her legs under the comforter, then lay back against the pillows. I walked to her and kissed her forehead, and then her lips.

"Sleep," I said.

She smiled and rolled onto her side. I turned the bedroom light off and pulled the door softly shut.

* * *

It was early enough that the town still slumbered as I went to the kitchen and poured a glass of water, dumping a package of dehydrated orange juice concentrate into it. I stirred the powder in the liquid until it was fully dissolved, then I lifted the glass and sipped. And swallowed.

It tasted like orange juice, but it was not. I set the glass on the counter and took the empty foil-lined pouch in hand. Some processing facility, likely on Hawaii, had filled it. Just as some ranch there had raised the cows and cattle which gave us milk and steak and leather goods. Pigs that rolled in muddy pens in the north fields had begun their lives at piglets on the island chain.

Now, that was all gone. Or enough of it to make the supply line we'd known, and depended upon, useless. If anyone was left in Hawaii, they were most certainly focused on their own survival in the face of a nuclear nightmare. In some ways, I wished that none would have to suffer through that. Maybe the blast the *Eisenhower* had delivered had been merciful. Maybe there were no scarred survivors.

Maybe.

We were still here, more alone than ever now. The *Rushmore* was gone with its base. There would be no more monthly deliveries to aid in our recovery. Bandon, for better or worse, was on its own.

Yes, I thought, there could be a better in the terrible situation. We would be forced to become fully self-sufficient, and to face the realities of that going forward.

"We're alone," Elaine said.

I turned to see her sitting in her chair in the doorway to the hall.

"That's what you're worried about," she added.

"It's only slightly freaky how well you know me," I said.

She wheeled herself to the counter and took my glass of orange juice, enjoying a sip for herself.

"Enjoy it while it lasts," I said.

The area surrounding Bandon was not optimal for growing citrus. If we wanted more of what Elaine and I were drinking, we would have to connect with some colony much farther south than we were. It was like that with many of the products we'd grown used to being provided. From this point on, it would be on us to make those things available.

"Maybe we can start a settlement in Florida," I said, holding the empty package up.

Elaine set the glass back on the counter.

"You know, Eric, for the first time in a long time, I'm..."

She hesitated, searching for the right words, I thought.

"What is it?" I asked.

"For the first time in a really long time, I'm worried about us."

I slid a chair from the table and sat, taking her hands in mine.

"I am, too," I said.

"What will Hope have when she gets older?" Elaine wondered aloud. "We have to make a future for her."

"We are," I assured her. "We will. This is a setback, but that's all. Everyone will just have to work harder, and smarter. But it will be worth it. Being truly self-sufficient will open up possibilities we can't even imagine now."

Elaine nodded, not disputing that, but somehow saddened by what it all would mean. For us. For everyone.

"We just won't be making that future here," she said.

"No," I said. "We won't."

Part Five

Spider and Fly

Thirty Three

I'd thought Elaine would wait. That she would let the events of the previous days fade from our immediate memory before acting.

She didn't.

"Your wife just dropped a bomb on the Town Council," Martin said through the screen door.

He stood on the porch, shifting his weight off and onto the leg he'd banged falling through the hole in the *Vinson's* hangar deck. It was just after noon, two days since he, and Schiavo, and I had returned aboard Chris Beekman's Cessna to a town that no one imagined would cease to exist. But that possibility, that suggestion, was precisely what Martin, in many ways the godfather of Bandon in the paternal sense, was referencing.

"I'll come out," I said.

Hope lay sleeping in her big girl bed, which had replaced the crib she'd known only a month earlier. She'd adjusted to napping without rails, though I found myself lining the edge of the mattress and the floor below with every spare pillow I could scrounge from other rooms. If, for some reason, she fussed, or woke and climbed out of bed, I would be able to hear from the porch.

I chose the chair nearest the door, and Martin the one next to it. At one time that had been where Elaine had sat, but, as my wife put it, she now came with her own seating.

"What happened?" I asked.

"I happened to be at the Town Hall while they were meeting," Martin said.

He was no longer part of the body that made decisions as to Bandon's governance. Neither was I. But each of us had spouses who were intimately involved in the running and protection of the town and its people.

"They took a break," Martin continued. "Angela came out and told me what Elaine had proposed. In essence, abandoning Bandon."

Martin might have expected some reaction right then. I offered none.

"It's an interesting idea of yours, Fletch."

I drew a breath and glanced back through the screen door, listening for Hope. It also gave me a moment to not react to my friend's very spot-on accusation.

"Fletch, Elaine didn't dream this up. She might have signed on, but this is you talking."

"What if it is?" I asked, looking back to Martin.

He smiled at my flourish of defensiveness.

"You didn't know she was going to bring it up, did you?"

I drew a breath and let the charged moment pass before shaking my head.

"That's a bit more than coming home to hear '*honey, I bought a couch*'," Martin joked.

He let out a light chuckle, as did I.

"I knew she'd embraced the whole thing pretty deeply," I said. "She took to the logic of it quickly, but..."

"You're not wrong," Martin said. "And neither is she."

For a moment we said nothing. We simply sat on the porch and gazed out at the neighborhood. A few people were out. Some strolling. Other tending to gardens.

Gardens...

"We have come a long way, Martin."

He was watching the same thing I was. The same activity that, for some time following the blight, none of us had expected to ever see again. Something so ordinary. Even mundane. Now, it was a scene of beauty. Of survival. Of defiance.

"Do you ever think that maybe all this, all of us being here, was meant to be?" I asked my friend.

"Some sort of destiny?" he asked, then shook his head. "We made this what it is. With sweat, and tears, and blood."

That we had. We'd all sacrificed, and we'd all lost so much. What Martin was expressing, I thought, was that whatever we'd all given up, it was a down payment on the future we all now had waiting for us.

If we did what was necessary to move toward that.

"Victim of our own success?" Martin posed the possibility to me.

"Not everyone who hears the rumors of a place called Bandon, a place where people live like this," I said, gesturing to my neighbor across the street picking berries from a bush in her front yard, "not all those people will see us as a place to join."

"A place to rule," Martin said, referencing the Unified Government's attempts to subjugate our town and its people.

"Or to destroy," I added.

Martin nodded and looked to me.

"If you were in there, Fletch, what would you be saying?"

I thought for a moment. It might have been just a curiosity he was expressing, or he might very well see whatever I had to say as some back-channel advice to his wife.

"Dividing up the population was Elaine's contribution to the idea," I said. "I have to agree with her, so I'd be proposing that we split up into at least ten new settlements. Eighty plus per settlement. Divide up the supplies, the seeds, everything, and get moving. We'd have to identify suitable towns to inhabit first, and none of them should be any closer than forty miles to the nearest neighbor. Maybe fifty."

"True separation," Martin observed. "You really want to spread out."

"If we're going to do this, we have to commit. It has to be for a purpose, and it has to serve that purpose."

"Survival," he said.

"To borrow from Elaine, get the eggs out of the same basket."

Martin nodded, both agreeing and not with the same gesture.

"Fletch..."

"Yes?"

"Micah."

That was all he said, and all he had to say. His child, the young soul who'd saved Bandon, and all who had come to it, and possibly the human race in its entirety, was buried in the town cemetery. His life had been too short, but his influence on the years that followed had been immeasurable. He was a touchstone to many.

And an anchor to his father.

"When Elaine came around to what I'd suggested, I turned into the doubter. I told her you couldn't force people to leave. That was true. But she reminded me that there was a better way—they would follow someone. The right person."

Martin's head tipped slightly downward, his gaze settling on the wooden porch floor.

"A lot of people still remember you as their leader," I said. "The town's leader. They're going to take whatever cue there is from you."

He looked to me now, a mix of sadness and apology in his eyes.

"I can't leave him," Martin said, his head shaking slightly, like a leaf disturbed by some faint breeze. "I just can't."

"You don't have to leave him forever," I said.

Martin seized on those words, a mix of confusion and possibility in his gaze.

"Someone will have to stay here," I said. "To fish, to run the petroleum processor. Not to mention the wells."

An infrastructure that supported Bandon had been built and maintained around it. These things could not all be loaded on the backs of trucks and hauled off to some new enclave.

"Bandon will just become another settlement," I said. "In time it will grow again, but so will the other places we plant our flag. It won't be the only shining light—just one among many."

"But if I stay..."

"Too many will stay with you," I said. "You have to leave. But that doesn't mean you can't visit. Someday, maybe, you could move back. You and Angela. Once Bandon is just that place that most everybody came from."

Martin stared at me and considered what I'd proposed for a moment. The impossibility of leaving his late son behind had seemed to dissolve away, replaced by a logical progression of events. Leave. Visit. Return. Only the first two were necessary to his signing onto the plan to scatter the population.

If that plan ever came to fruition at all.

Thirty Four

Elaine brought the suppressed MP5 up and snugged it against her shoulder, her cheek tipping toward the extended stock. The sights lined up as she looked down the top of the receiver and barrel. She drew a breath, released it slowly, and squeezed the trigger.

A quick burst of 9mm rounds spat from the end of the slender suppressor, fire pulsing and muted cracks sounding. Fifty feet from her a pair of cans arranged atop an old fencepost spun into the air, tumbling to the ground as the row of dead pines behind them erupted with a shower of blighted grey dust.

She adjusted her aim as I watched from behind, directing more fire into the fallen cans, each dancing further off into the woods with each barrage she put into them. When her magazine ran dry she removed it and safed the compact submachinegun before looking to me, a pleased grin on her face.

I held out a fresh mag to her, the last of the five I'd filled before our trip to the shooting range just east of town. She waved off the offer and handed me her weapon and the spent magazine.

"That felt good," she said.

Two cans. Three jugs of water. Some old hunks of driftwood. She'd expertly blasted each into oblivion.

"You needed it," I said, setting the MP5 on the open tailgate of our pickup. "You've needed it for a while."

Two years it had been since she'd had any trigger time. The last time she'd held her preferred weapon was the day she'd lost the use of her legs. She'd always been highly proficient with it, and practiced regularly, but in the time since that last battle against the Unified Government forces there hadn't seemed much point in it. That, at least, was what I imagined she thought.

But with the burden now placed upon her as leader of Bandon, and especially with the momentous proposal being considered, if nothing else, she deserved some plain old stress relief in the form of the free application of firepower against inanimate objects.

She reached out and took the MP5 in hand once more, its magazine well empty. For a minute, she just held the weapon, testing its weight. Reacquainting herself with it.

"I was pretty good with this thing," she said.

"For a stubby little gun, yeah, you were."

She smiled at me, but the expression lasted just a few seconds.

"I remember wondering when I became an FBI agent if I'd ever have to take a life in the line of duty," Elaine said. "That seems like such a quaint thought now. I mean, how many lives have I taken since the world went to hell? Is there any way to even know?"

I didn't know why that nagging curiosity had risen right then. On occasion I'd wondered the same thing myself. How many people had I killed? More unsettling, though, was the reality that the question could be asked at all. In a normal life, when such things were possible, the answer would almost universally be '*zero*'. But we'd left '*normal*' in our dust long ago.

"No," I said. "But every life you took saved one that mattered. Either you, or me, or someone else."

She didn't doubt my response. Nor did she dwell on what the answer might mean for her.

"It was just a stray thought," she said, laying the MP5 back on the tailgate. "I hadn't used that for anything other than killing in a long time."

The killing, maybe, was done now. And the dying. I truly wanted to believe that.

"What will Martin do?" she asked me.

I'd told her of his visit. And his hesitation. And, maybe, his acceptance of what was being discussed behind closed doors. But, when the moment came to actually decide, only he knew what path he would choose.

"I don't know," I told her.

"He has every reason to stay."

"He does," I agreed with my wife. "What about her?"

"Angela?"

I nodded. After Martin had left, the part she would play in his decision began to percolate in my thoughts.

"The garrison is here," I said. "Do they stay together? Does she split them up?"

"That will be part of the discussion," Elaine said.

The Town Council would continue debating and deciding on Bandon's fate as a community when they reconvened the next morning. When any consensus on a plan would be reached was still unknown.

"It's more than just her," Elaine said. "You split the garrison, but what about Clay Genesee?"

There was no longer any illusion that he was *Commander* Genesee, United States Navy. He'd formally resigned, inasmuch as that was possible, by handing a letter to Schiavo shortly after he and Grace had said 'I do' to each other. Still, he was the only actual physician left after the passing of Doc Allen. A capable cadre of nurses, led by Grace, as well as the garrison's medic, Sergeant Trey Hart, rounded out the medical staff which had kept the town's residents alive through injuries and illness.

"People have traveled to see doctors before," I reminded her. "If he's centrally located, it's a two-hour drive from one of the settlements. Fifteen minutes by air if necessary."

"I know all that," she said. "It's just convincing people that that sort of arrangement will be workable is not a slam dunk."

"None of this is," I said.

"Yeah. In some ways, it's the hardest thing we've had to do."

"You know why?"

"Not entirely."

"Because we're creating the unknown," I said.

I wasn't a man prone to bouts of profound thought, or words, but I was fairly certain that I'd described the situation with accurate brevity. If only the solution were as easy to express.

"Let's go pick up our little girl, Mr. Philosopher," Elaine said, ribbing me as she wheeled herself to the passenger door.

I stowed the weapon and gear and locked the tailgate up, then climbed behind the wheel just as Elaine expertly swung her chair into the back and joined me in the cab.

"Have you thought about where we should go?" Elaine asked.

"I haven't," I told her as I started the pickup and pulled away from the firing range.

"After all the places we've scouted and been, you don't have any preference?"

"No," I said.

"If this all goes through, we're going to have to make that decision," she said.

I steered from the dirt track back onto the road that would take us to town.

"That time will come then," I said.

She puzzled at me for a minute or two as we neared the edge of Bandon. Then, as the buildings and the newly grown trees and the people out for walks came into view, she understood. She knew.

I didn't want to think about leaving yet. Even though it had been my idea which had sparked the possibility of this place becoming just a memory for us, that didn't erase the true, affectionate connection I felt for all that was here.

"I'm going to miss it, too, Eric."

I glanced to her and smiled. She undid her seatbelt and slid across the bench seat and sat next to me, head leaning on my shoulder, comforting me with her presence as we drove into the town that we called home. For now.

Thirty Five

The Town Council discussed the proposal for three days. Rumblings of what was being considered began to ripple through the town's population. Calls even came in from Remote asking what was happening. There was gossip. Theories. Outright lies. Accusations.

Mostly, though, there was fear. Uncertainty. The life everyone had fought for was being branded a danger, most felt, without the life they would have to make in a new place coming with any guarantees of safety and prosperity. At a town meeting called to clear the air and give the residents facts, it was that very fear which began to overwhelm the gathering.

"There are none," I said, loud enough to be heard over the voices challenging the Town Council members who, mostly, stood before those they served. "No guarantees."

I'd stayed off to the side of the gathering, which was being held in the cool afternoon air outside the old meeting hall, its confines turned into a storage space for all manner of supplies. Bandon's junk drawer, it had become. But the memories of momentous discussions and decisions which had been made within were still fresh in most minds. As were memories of who had made those decisions.

"Martin, are you going along with this?"

The challenge was nearly shouted at the town's former leader as he stood just behind me, all eyes shifting from Schiavo and Elaine and the others who had assumed the mantle of government, and back to the man who, in practical purposes, had been a dictator without force. People had listened to him, had followed his edicts, because those actions on his part had kept them alive in the most trying times.

Now, in this time, a clear majority of those in attendance were looking to him again, for the same guidance he had once offered.

"I can't tell you what to do," Martin said.

I could sense it as he spoke those words, the crowd's resurgent hope in his leadership deflating. He wasn't giving them what they wanted.

He was, however, giving them what they needed.

"I can tell you that I will be moving on," Martin added. "Angela and I will be making a new home wherever this journey takes us."

I glanced to the members of the Town Council. Schiavo, an advisor to the body, allowed a slight smile at what her husband had just said. Seated in her wheelchair next to the town's senior military officer, my wife was less overt in her appreciation toward Martin. A broad, almost uncharacteristic smile was spread across her face, as though some great weight had just been lifted from her. From all of them.

Which it had.

* * *

Residents gathered in knots to discuss what they'd just heard once the meeting ended. Some peppered those who'd brought the proposal to them with questions in a more intimate setting. When all that had subsided, there were just the four of us left, standing near our cars a block away from the meeting hall, one Humvee and one old pickup.

"You know anyone who's looking to sell one of those?" Martin asked.

"A pickup?" I asked.

"Yeah," he said. "Bill Powers was working on a couple he scavenged, if I remember correctly."

"He is, yeah," I said.

I was slightly confused. Unless Martin wanted the hassle of a vehicle to maintain on his own, I couldn't understand why he, or they, needed anything more than the Humvee assigned permanently to Schiavo.

Then, I understood. The Humvee wasn't assigned to her—it was attached to the office. The commander of the garrison.

That smile at the airfield after we'd landed had been about more than happiness at our survival. It had come from a place of deeper satisfaction. Of decision.

"Do you have something to announce?" I asked Schiavo.

She thought for a moment, then shook her head.

"I've discussed it with Elaine," she said.

I looked to my wife, offering her a raised eyebrow.

"I don't have to tell you everything," she said, grinning.

"Obviously," I said.

"People are going to want to vote on the proposal," Schiavo said. "After that I can make my intentions known."

Colonel Schiavo, whom I'd met as Lieutenant Schiavo in the battle on Mary Island, was going to shed all those terms before her given name, Angela, and join the ranks of civilian life.

"Paul is ready," she said, offering clear praise to her second in command, Lieutenant Paul Lorenzen, who'd been in operational command of the garrison for some time now.

"I know he is," I said. "But are you?"

She smiled a shrug.

"Don't know," she said, leaning against Martin like a high school girl close to her crush. "But it's time."

We'd all lived several lifetimes since the blight exploded across the globe. Done more, seen more, than most would ever have in a single lifetime in the old world.

Angela Schiavo most certainly deserved a chance at a life that did not involve camouflage and command.

"You want me to call Bill and see if he's got a truck ready for sale?" I asked.

Martin shook his head.

"I'll give him a call," he said. "Soon."

That time would come, he knew. But, for now, his wife still did wear mottled green and black, and did have to make decisions that could end in life or death for so many. He didn't want to jump the gun, because she didn't, I knew. She was a pro, and always had been.

And always would be.

Thirty Six

We had a week of spring left. And then summer. By fall, those who would be moving on from Bandon had to be in their new settlements. In houses which were ready for them. With enough infrastructure to provide for them before the ultimate deadline.

Winter.

Despite the time crunch, though, the numbers were impressive. Following the meeting where Martin shared his intentions, a survey was completed. A test of the town's acceptance of the proposal. To say that the results were surprising was an understatement.

"Ninety two percent," Elaine announced in the Town Hall conference room. "Ninety two percent agree with the proposal."

She looked to me, and to Schiavo, and to Martin. We were there with Dave Arndt, the five of us having accepted appointment to what was being called the Resettlement Committee. On our shoulders the challenge of deciding exactly how, and where, to move the population rested. And now we had an idea of just how many people that would entail.

"Seventy or so don't want to go," Martin said, thinking. "Another hundred will have to stay here to operate the fishing fleet, the oil wells, a scaled-back ranching and farming operation."

"Just under two hundred will remain," Elaine said.

"That leaves about seven hundred who'll be part of the move," Dave said.

"Ten settlements of seventy," I said.

The number hung there for a moment as each of us considered the possibility. And the difficulties.

"Is that doable?" Dave wondered. "Prepping ten new towns? I mean, essentially that's what we're talking about. Making ten towns ready for human occupancy."

That was what we were talking about. Some pieces of the puzzle that would allow such a scattered endeavor were already in place, and would remain so. Remote's greenhouse operation would provide the plants and seeds for every new settlement. Just up the road from them, Camas Valley would be called upon to build more batteries, more solar and wind generators, and more electric vehicles to outfit these far flung outposts. Much, though, would have to be done on the fly.

Figuratively and literally.

"We need to find those towns first," I reminded everyone.

Elaine nodded and looked to Dave Arndt.

"Don't you two have a plane to catch?"

Thirty Seven

We cruised in the surviving Cessna at a thousand feet above the ground, Dave piloting the aircraft up and down to follow the rise and fall of the terrain below.

"Isn't this how this all started, Fletch?"

I looked to Dave from the passenger seat and adjusted the headset's boom microphone closer to my lips.

"How so?"

"You and me, up in a plane, when that signal came out of nowhere."

He was right. And that wasn't some ancient event. It was two weeks ago, now.

"Let's just make this an uneventful trip," I said.

Dave smiled and nodded, his attention focused out the windshield, the midday sun laying sparkles across the glass. All the protection that Chris Beekman had added to the aircraft, a hundred pounds or more of fine metal mesh, had been removed, extending the range at which we could survey the landscape below.

We weren't searching in the blind, however. On my lap was a map with circles around towns to scan from the air. Places which, if they were habitable, would fit the criteria that had been established.

No settlement could be closer than roughly forty-five miles as the crow flew from the nearest other settlement. Taken to its extreme, that meant that, theoretically, a string of ten settlements could stretch out four hundred and fifty miles from Bandon. More likely, though, these newly occupied towns would exist in a widely spread cluster stretching mostly south and southeast from where we'd taken off. The reason for that was obvious as we looked to the earth below.

"Hard to believe how stark that line is," Dave commented.

It was that. Black turning to grey as we flew on a southeast heading, passing over the area where the volcanic ash from the eruption of Mount Hood still painted the landscape dark. Where the southernmost reach of the ash cloud ended, the familiar canvas of blighted grey began, forests withered and toppling.

"Look at all that fertilizer," I said.

At first the ash cloud had been devastating, though Bandon had escaped the worst of it. But as the months passed and the rains came, what the volcano had spewed had become a welcome amendment to the soil. In all the dead land below, when life again did spread its way, trees and berry bushes and run of the mill weeds would find hospitable earth ready to accept and nourish their roots.

"Yeah," Dave said. "And then there's all that."

The dead zone. The grey world. I'd trudged back and forth across half the country through the gritty, colorless dust that was cast off from every dying pine or blade of grass. It was a sickening sight then, and it was no less so now. The new growth, the return of greens and yellows and purples, had spread from Bandon over the past three years, so much so that little evidence of the blighted woods remained within sight of town. And what did remain was slated to be bulldozed.

Or would have been.

There still would be seeding in and around Bandon. That process would not stop. It could not stop. But the pace would have to slow as seeds and saplings were transferred to each of the new settlements. The vision was no longer a single place of greenery, but, rather, a spreading patchwork of life across the landscape as we reclaimed more of the earth. And secured ourselves in the process.

"Were you surprised that Chris didn't want to pilot this mission?" I asked Dave.

"I think he's more focused on replacing the plane he lost."

My pilot was right about that. Chris Beekman, almost immediately after returning from our successful mission to the carrier, had begun scouting locations where more salvageable small planes might exist. A flight south had led him to what he was looking for. At an airfield across the border in California, just inland from Crescent City, he'd spotted a trio of abandoned aircraft, two Cessnas and a twin-engine Piper. All looked to be in rough shape, and the runway at what was called Ward Field was unusable, Beekman reported. A road trip would be required to reach their location and give them a closer look.

"I told him if he's able to get any of them airworthy, I'd want to talk about buying one from him."

"Looking to start a charter business, Dave?" I asked my friend.

"Maybe," he said. "I also think we're going to be doing a lot of short hops between all these new settlements."

"You're gonna be a busy man if Chris hands the keys over to you."

"He's gotta get 'em into the air first," Dave reminded me.

That part of Chris Beekman's plan was underway as we spoke. With the overland trip approved by both Elaine and Schiavo, Beekman had headed out a few hours before we'd taken off. With him were Sergeants Enderson and Hart, Will Sherman who did odd jobs around the airport for Beekman, and two Humvees with extra fuel and special trailering hitches installed. The plan was, if the planes were found to be repairable, the wings would be removed, strapped lengthwise to the fuselages, and each aircraft would be towed back to Bandon.

"If all three are worth salvaging, how hard do you think it will be for Chris to only come home with two?" I asked.

"That'll just mean another trip to—"

Dave's answer ended abruptly and he leaned forward, rising a bit from his seat, as far as the safety restraints would allow, so that he could see past the nose of the aircraft. Past and below.

"Fletch..."

I was already looking, searching for what might have caught Dave's eye. It only took a few seconds to spot what he had. Missing it was impossible.

"Green," I said.

"A lot of green," Dave added.

206 Noah Mann

Thirty Eight

Dead ahead of us, on a patch of earth bordered by a road on the south, was a swath of that color. That hue of life amidst a grey world.

"Those are trees," Dave said. "Live trees."

"I know," I said. "That's gotta be ten acres or more."

"Where are we?" he asked, scanning the terrain ahead. "Is that Klamath falls up there."

"Yeah," I answered, checking the map. "There's an airport there."

Dave looked to me, more than a hint of surprise about him.

"You want to set down?"

"That's life down there, Dave. It's worth checking out."

We were forty miles from the survivor colony that had been located in Northern California near Hornbrook, and eighty miles south of Clearwater, far inland from Bandon, where the other band of survivors been discovered. Neither of those groups had reported contact with anyone from the area around Klamath Falls.

"We haven't scouted this area," Dave reminded me.

"Exactly. What if they've been here all along?"

Dave looked again as we passed to the south of the area of interest, just off our left wingtip as he put the Cessna into a wide orbit around the uneven patch of living foliage.

"But Fletch, that's not just some people. Stuff is growing down there. Stuff is *alive*. How is that possible?"

"How is it possible that everything around Bandon is green now?" I asked him. "Maybe we're not the only ones who found the answer."

He nodded, but wasn't fully convinced.

"You think it's a good idea?" he pressed.

"If we don't, it's just going to mean another trip out here," I told him. "We'll eventually have to make contact with whoever's down there."

"I suppose, if it all checks out, this wouldn't be a bad place for one of our settlements," Dave said, warming to the idea. "If there's already some sort of presence there, and things growing, our people would have a leg up on making it work."

"Right," I said, pointing to the south as Dave made another orbit. "The airport is about three miles east of the Klamath River."

Dave shook his head at that information, and the suggestion that accompanied it.

"This spot is another two miles to the river," he said. "That's a five-mile walk. And we'd have to leave the plane behind. Unprotected."

I knew what Dave was thinking without him needing to say it.

"You think you can land on one of these roads?"

He nodded and pointed to a straight stretch of blacktop that ran directly toward the area of greenery. It was free of wrecks and other obstacles, mostly fields to either side.

"No obstructions, and plenty long enough for landing and takeoff," he said. "That's two thousand feet easy, and I only need a bit over fifteen hundred."

Leaving the Cessna behind, unattended and unprotected, was not a great idea, I had to admit. But I was equally unsure of the novice pilot's ability to land on surface not intended for that.

"Fletch, the guy who landed you on an aircraft carrier taught me how to fly," Dave assured me. "I can do this. Really."

One of us was a capable pilot with over a hundred hours at the controls, and the other guy was me.

"All right," I told Dave. "Let's go have a look."

Dave keyed the mic button on the yoke.

"BC, this is SF Two, do you copy?"

There was only soft static in response. The hiss of dead air.

"BC, do you read?"

"We're awful far with terrain between us," I said.

His attempt to notify those back home of our plan was logical, but likely impossible. There simply was no line of sight between us and the receiving station in town.

"Bandon Center, this is Scouting Flight Two, we are landing near Klamath Falls to investigate a possible survivor colony."

Again, there was no reply.

"Just wanted to give it a shot," Dave said, then ceased his efforts at communication. "I'm gonna swing around and have a look before lining us up."

He performed the maneuver smoothly, banking over the Klamath River before leveling out with our intended landing strip dead ahead. From the map I could see that it was a stretch of asphalt named Balsam Drive, farmland and farmhouses sparse to either side. Food had once been plentiful here. Things grown. Animals raised. Perhaps, somehow, enough people had hung on until the cure for the blight had, somehow, reached them.

Or, had they come across an entirely different way to defeat the scourge which had ravaged the earth.

"We've got clear air and minimal obstructions," Dave reported as he did a low pass over the road.

"Those wires won't be a problem?"

"Halfway down the landing and takeoff run," he said. "We'll be on the ground passing under them."

More electrical wires had, at one time, crossed the road at several places. But time, weather, and neglect had brought the poles supporting them down. Or, possibly, survivors not long after the blight struck had taken them down for firewood. That was the time of scavenging and scavengers, taking what was necessary to stay alive.

"Wires on the road won't snag the wheels?" I asked.

"I don't see any, Fletch."

Those lengths of copper and steel wire might have been valuable to someone at the time. Or even to those who now tended the greenery that had drawn us to this place.

"We have power," I said. "No reason to think they wouldn't, I guess."

Power required wire to distribute. This, and what we'd seen from the air, pointed to a group of survivors who weren't just scratching for scraps to stay alive. They'd found a way to actually live. To sustain themselves.

And now, we'd found them.

"Turning for final approach," Dave said.

He nosed the Cessna up, gaining altitude and turning toward the river again, executing the sweeping turn for his final approach. There would be no low pass this time. We were going to see up close just who had carved out an existence in the hills at the end of the road.

"Fifty feet," Dave said as we slowed and settled toward the road. "Twenty. Ten. Five."

The wheels screeching as they spun suddenly on the pavement announced our touchdown. We rolled down the unmaintained road, bouncing over potholes and deep gouges where the blacktop had been ripped away. But nothing made it impassable, and just past a collapsed farmhouse where an intersecting road split off to the north, Dave slowed and swung the Cessna until it was pointing the way we'd come, now ready for departure. He set the brakes and shut the engine off.

"Let's see who our neighbors might be," Dave said, slipping out of his headset.

I removed mine as well and released my seatbelt, opening the passenger door and stepping out with my M4 in hand and my Kimber on my hip. Both had replaced my preferred weapons, which had been lost when we were captured aboard the carrier. I felt completely comfortable with my new personal arsenal, both rifle and pistol nearly identical platforms when compared with what I'd lost. Neither, I hoped, would be seeing any use on this scouting mission, but they, and I, had to be ready.

Yes, whoever was up the road might be our neighbors, our fellow survivors, but they were still an unknown.

And we'd learned, more than once, just how that void of information could turn to disaster with little warning.

Thirty Nine

We left the Cessna behind and walked toward the hills.

A quarter mile up Balsam Drive a road split off to the right, leading to the area we'd seen from the air. We walked alongside each other, Dave on the right edge of the road with his Remington 12 gauge, and me on the left, my M4 held low but ready.

"It's awful quiet, Fletch."

I nodded. We'd begun to forget just how silent the blighted world was. Bandon had moved beyond all that, to point where conversations and car engines and the occasional bird tweeting no longer seemed odd. This, what Dave and I were experiencing, *did* seem odd. Sound odd.

Feel odd.

"I half expected a welcoming committee," Dave said. "They had to have seen and heard us fly over."

"They have no idea if we're friend or foe, Dave. We might hide, too."

He accepted that with a nod and stayed focused. I remained vigilant, too, because, though I wouldn't say it to Dave right then, there was that *feeling*. It was a sensation that we were not alone, but, also, that we might not be welcome.

"I see the treetops," Dave said.

Ahead, further up the hill, beyond the stands of dead pine and fir trees, living members of their species stood, green tips standing out above the grey and crumbling woods.

"Let's go off road to the north," I suggested.

Dave led off without being asked, blazing a path to the right over fields where grass had once stood tall. Just dirt and the remnants of withered twigs and thick stalks remained, crushing to dust beneath our boots. We crossed this open space and entered the woods, ashen trunks rising all around us, snapped limbs scattered about the forest floor.

"Why haven't they cleared this?" Dave wondered aloud.

"I don't know," I said, searching for that very answer myself. "A buffer? Camouflage? They want to stay hidden from the road."

Dave accepted those suggestions with a shrug. It was possible the survivors somewhere ahead hadn't anticipated being spotted from the air. This was not a world where technological wonders, like airplanes, still existed in any numbers to be of a concern. They simply might have been unprepared for the possibility. That could also add credence to their reluctance to openly greet us.

"Should we call out?" Dave asked.

"Give it a try," I said.

We paused between two old, dead lodgepole pines, still surrounded by the grey woods, the place of new growth still a few hundred yards ahead.

"Hello!" Dave shouted. "We saw you from the air! We're from Bandon! On the coast! We're here to help!"

For a moment we listened, and we heard nothing. Only the gentle breeze that seemed to fill so many of the empty spaces away from the civilization we'd begun to rebuild.

"Camas Valley hid from us, too," I reminded Dave.

That group of survivors, advanced in their development, had only become known after the settlement at Remote had been established. Proximity, and a willingness to open up, had exposed them. We had no idea what the survivors nearby, in this place, had been through to make them hide from contact.

"We're not an enemy!" Dave added. "Please come out!"

Still there was no response.

"Let's keep moving," I said.

That feeling I'd had was changing. The lack of open contact, of greeting, was adding a fair dose of wariness to what was working on me. The unknown was becoming more of a concern, and less of a curiosity.

"We could just head out if you're not sure," Dave said.

I shook my head. We were already here, and whatever my gut feeling was, it needed to be backed up by some evidence. Some indication of trouble. But there was none. All that we'd experienced so far were empty woods and silence.

"Let's check out the growth at least," I said.

If those who'd tended the greenery didn't wish to be found, we could not force them to show themselves. But we could at least lay eyes on what they'd managed to grow where nothing had for many years.

"Got it," Dave said.

We pressed on, walking abreast, a few yards between us as we weaved slowly through the dead trees, slowing, and finally stopping when what we'd come to see lay just before us. Except...

"Fletch, those trees aren't alive."

Dave was right. I looked at them, up and down, and at the low shrubs that filled a clearing just beyond them. A few more steps took me to one of the pines and I put my hand against the trunk, which was as green as the limbs. When I pulled it away my palm was stained a bright, unnatural green.

"It's paint," I said.

Forty

Dave reached out and dragged his hand across one of the shrubs. It came back covered in the exact wet hue as mine.

"It's all paint," he said.

He began to back away.

"Fresh paint," he added.

"Let's get out of—"

I never got the last word out. The sharp crack of the rifle shot ended any need for the warning. Worse, it left me with no one to warn.

The bullet, which had been fired from our front, somewhere in the cover beyond the faux greenery, struck Dave Arndt square in the forehead. An explosion of blood and things I didn't want to think of sprayed from the back of his head as the high velocity round exited. His body collapsed almost straight down, like a puppet who'd lost its puppeteer.

I spun away, covered in what had been blasted from my friend's head, and took cover behind the painted pine. Suddenly there were sounds in the woods now. Movement. Words. Directives.

Get him...

Waiting was no option. I pushed off and sprinted away, jerking left and right through the grey woods that hid what was very plainly a trap. One that had lured us in.

Us...

There was no more 'us'. There was only me. And I had to get out of what was clearly the kill zone. Shots rang out behind me as I moved. Bullets ripped into the trees to either side. Five separate shooters were taking aim at me, I could tell. All squeezing off single shots. Conserving ammunition with aimed fire.

My choice was to press on, maintaining a fast pace as I fled, or to pause and return fire. I chose the former. For now, at least. I needed to get away from my pursuers and back to...

The plane.

It might as well have been a speedboat. Either would have done me as much good as the other parked on that road. I was not capable of flying the Cessna. I didn't even know how to start the aircraft. At best it was a thin-skinned coffin for me.

Think, Fletch...

I tried as I ran and dodged the fire chasing me. There were a hundred and fifty miles between me and home, if I could fly. It was easily over two hundred by any land route I could manage.

Except I could manage none. The only supplies I had were back at the plane, a survival kit in the baggage compartment meant to last us three days. That would be six days for one person, now.

Focus...

There was only one priority. Not getting to the plane. Not getting home. Getting to safety was the only thing that mattered at the moment.

I spun fast and fired three bursts, one in each slice of the pie behind me, hoping the attack would be slowed by my resistance. It wasn't.

More weapons opened up on me, from the sides now, rounds impacting the trees ahead. I changed course, ducking, struggling to avoid the incoming fire. Moving due north now I slid down a small slope through the monolithic grey woods, the pursuers still behind me. Driving me forward. I fired more bursts, but they were not deterred. That was not the worst realization right then, though.

"No..."

The woods which had afforded me some cover ended ahead, spilling into an open expanse of dirty earth stretching hundreds of yards down the hillside. I would be totally exposed.

This is it...

I stopped where the last line of trees was and turned back, my M4 up, scanning the forest I'd just raced through. Shapes flitted about in the cover I'd left behind. I squeezed off two bursts, then dropped the empty magazine and inserted a fresh one, pushing the bolt forward to continue the fight.

It turned out, I fired no more shots that day.

"You're surrounded, Fletch," the man's voice said. "We have people across the field."

The nearest cover, several hundred yards across the slope, was another patch of dead woods. It was too far for me to make out any hostiles amongst those trees, but I had no reason to doubt what I was being told. We'd walked into a perfectly set ambush. We'd taken the bait laid for us. One of us had paid with his life. I wondered if I was about to.

"Last chance, Fletch."

Beyond the tactical disadvantage I was at, the man speaking was addressing me by name. He knew me. And I had to admit, with each word he spoke, I believed I knew exactly who he was.

"What do you want, Perkins?!"

Earl Perkins. Leader of the Yuma survivor colony which had aligned itself with the Unified Government. That entity, presumably, existed no more. But somehow Perkins and, it seemed, some of his followers, had managed to hang on after being cut off from the supply chain our side had enjoyed.

But it had been years since we'd had any contact with the officious, arrogant turncoat. How had he survived and made his way north? That might have been a very valid question, but another which came to mind, 'why', I could imagine an easy answer for.

He was coming for Bandon. What the Unified Government military had failed to do, Earl Perkins, and whatever force he had with him, was going to try to complete.

"Fletch, you had a chance to sign on with me long ago," Perkins shouted through the woods. "This is the very last chance I'm giving you to stay alive."

If I'd known where he stood amongst the shadows between the trees, I might have used what ammunition I had left to fire a final volley his way. It would be a suicide mission, but, if successful, the satisfaction might have been worth the price I'd pay.

That was fantasy, though. In this very real moment of decision that I faced, my life hung in the balance. I could make my stand and die or live to fight another day.

Maybe.

I had to take the chance, no matter the consequences. I rose slowly behind the tree, which was the only cover I had, and brought my M4 up, then tossed it out into the open.

"Now your sidearm," Perkins said. "Do you still have that Springfield you liked so much, Fletch?"

I didn't. The pistol that replaced it slid from my holster, likely for the last time. With a gentle throw it sailed off and landed next to my rifle.

"Anything else, Fletch?" Perkins asked, a smug politeness in his manner. "We don't want to find some hideout piece when we search you."

Hideout piece...

The man had watched too many bad detective shows when there were such things. He probably believed that a thump on the head from a pistol butt would simply knock an adversary out, and not cause a likely fatal subdural hematoma. But that was what I remembered of Perkins—he was a man of shallow intellect paired with a broad sense of self.

"I don't have one, Perkins!"

"Drop all your gear and step out into the clear," Perkins ordered.

There was more movement to the woods on either side of me. His people were closing in for the kill if I didn't cooperate.

It was time to face my reality.

"All right!"

I shed my belt and holster and backed away from the tree, my hands held up. Within seconds a dozen fighters emerged from the woods, their mix of weapons aimed at me. Shotguns, ARs, AKs, bolt actions, pistols. And one crossbow. If they wanted me dead, that's exactly what would happen.

But they didn't. Or, rather, *he* didn't.

"Eric Fletcher," Earl Perkins said as he stepped out from cover and onto the sloped clearing. "Fletch himself."

The diminutive autocrat walked toward me and stopped, regarding me with a grin that was both satisfied and surprised.

"Who was your friend, Fletch?" Perkins asked.

Was...

For a few minutes as I'd fled from the pursuit, I'd let thoughts of Dave Arndt fade, masked by tactical and practical considerations. Now, though, I was thinking of my friend again.

"He was a good man," I told Perkins. "That's who he was."

The grin faded. I hadn't offered a direct answer to the question posed. I had shown a sign of resistance. Of disrespect. All quite intentional.

And I was going to pay for it.

Perkins drew a long revolver from the holster he wore diagonal on the front of his belt and whipped its thick barrel across my face. After the pummeling I'd experienced aboard the *Vinson*, the hit felt amplified, as though I'd been struck by two men twice Perkins' size. I spun to the side and fell to my hands and knees.

"Get on your feet," Perkins ordered me.

I hesitated and looked up to the man, but he was having none of my resistance.

"Get him up," he told his followers.

A pair of men, thin and muscular, grabbed me and held me up, facing Perkins.

"Strip that shirt off and search him, Bryce," he instructed one of the men. "Then get him on my truck."

Hands pulled at my clothes and probed my pockets as Perkins turned and walked away through the woods, a half dozen of his followers in tow. Others gathered my weapons and gear before my hands were tied, but not behind my back or in front. Instead they were bound together at the back of my neck, with a loop of rough rope circling my throat.

"He's clean," one of the people said after finishing their check of me.

"Let's go," the one called Bryce said, some clear authority about him. "Get him to the boss's ride."

The hands that had rifled through my clothing now seized me by my upturned arms and forced me back up the hill through the trees, marching me past Dave Arndt's body. His fate had been decided and played out. The only hope I had was that, right then, mine was not.

Forty One

The convoy of vehicles left the road next to the woods and drove back to Balsam Drive and turned toward Klamath Falls.

One vehicle was ahead and one behind the flatbed truck that carried me. I'd been lashed to a steel roll bar behind the cab, facing backwards so that I faced Perkins. He sat in an upholstered lounge chair that had been bolted to the truck bed. It had all the appearances of a cheap throne.

"So what was all that noise?" Perkins asked me from his chair. "We couldn't hear you guys for a while."

The jamming. His group had heard it because they'd been listening to us. Monitoring our communications. Listening to our plans.

"You knew we were scouting this area today," I said.

Perkins grinned, one corner of his mouth twitching upward. He brought an imaginary mic to his mouth.

"Uh, Camas Valley, will you tune your repeater for southern reception in the morning," he mocked. "We have a scouting flight heading out toward Klamath Falls tomorrow."

He lowered his hand and laughed fully now.

"You think the world is an inherently safe place now," he said. "You can just scatter the sweet folks of Bandon to this spot here, or that spot there, and you'll all be the better for it."

Bryce, standing next to me, chuckled as he gripped the roll bar with one hand and his shotgun with the other.

"Fletch, for a community which has lasted this long, you're all fairly naïve," Perkins commented. "You have to be strong, and stay strong, and you have to be willing to project that strength if you want to stick around."

"Your point, Perkins?" I challenged him.

"You don't divide your people," he said. "The people are power. Dilute that, and you have nothing."

"You're coming here to save us from ourselves, Perkins? Is that it?"

"I didn't think I was," he said. "No, Fletch, this was supposed to be a pure revenge play. My intent was to destroy."

"General Weatherly tried," I reminded him. "Him, his troops, they all turned to fish food."

"Weatherly was a soldier," Perkins said, dismissing that classification with a shake of his head. "Believe it or not, my friend, he had a code of honor. Enemies can subscribe to such quaint notions, you know."

"But you don't."

Perkins leaned forward in his green fabric throne and almost sneered at me.

"I'm a *leader*, Fletch. A man willing to do anything to see that my people survive. Through strength and discipline."

"You're quite the little dictator," I said.

Ignoring the motion of the flatbed, Perkins shot up from his chair and charged at me, grabbing my throat with his bare hand, fingertips digging painfully into the flesh.

"Talk is easy, my friend," he growled. "You know what isn't?"

I had no answer for him, and wouldn't have bothered even if I had.

"I returned to Yuma from that fiasco in Alaska with a hundred and change," he said. "Less than two hundred people. By the time the Unified Government showed up, we'd grown to three hundred. When we left six months ago, four hundred followed me."

Was he suggesting that the entire Yuma survivor colony had up and left, on his orders, to come here?

"Surprise," he said, mocking my obvious reaction. "That, Fletch, is what a leader does. And do you know how many are still with me? Right now?"

This time I managed a slight shake of my head against the grip he still had on my neck.

"All...of...them."

He let go of me and returned to his chair as the flatbed slowed and rumbled off the road, using the space of a barren farm field to skirt the spot we'd landed. Perkins looked to the Cessna as we eased past it, a group of his people already poring over it, attaching a tow strap to the nose wheel strut.

"Air power," Perkins said. "What do you know, Bryce—we have an air force now."

"Yes we do," Bryce agreed. "We can mount some machine guns on it. Have a real warbird."

Perkins smiled at me.

"I have four people who can fly," he said to me. "Three more planes and I'll have a squadron."

"Are you actually thinking you can attack Bandon?" I asked. "We've faced worse than you. A bigger force than you. Our population is over twice your number."

"Long odds, you think," Perkins said.

"Suicide odds, Perkins. And you know that."

"Do I?"

We bounced back onto the road and picked up speed, heading east toward Klamath Falls.

"You, Fletch, are missing one key piece of information."

"And what is that?"

Perkins reclined in his cushioned throne and beamed, more satisfied with himself than he'd ever been, I suspected.

"My secret weapon," he said.

Forty Two

Our three vehicle convoy pulled into town, stopping in front of an old motel, its signage toppled onto the sidewalk out front. The wide avenue we'd come to looked no different than any of the deserted thoroughfares in any of the countless towns I'd passed through in the wake of the blight. Broken windows. Scattered, rotting furnishings in the street. Dust blowing in the breeze.

"What do you think, Fletch?" Perkins asked.

"I love what you've done with it," I said.

Perkins smiled at my insolence this time, then nodded to Bryce, who thumped his fist on the top of the cab. A second later the vehicle's horn sounded, three long blasts. When the last one had faded to silence, the town, slowly, came to what passed for life.

From trashed stores and abandoned motel rooms, people emerged. Men. Women, Children. They were haggard and thin, but they stood straight. Every man carried a weapon, and most of the women as well. The smallest children hugged stuffed animals and toys soiled by years of use or persistent neglect.

"Get him down," Perkins ordered.

He climbed down and stood next to the flatbed as Bryce cut me loose from the roll bar, my arms still lashed awkwardly behind my head. Two others, a man and a woman, approached, and Bryce passed me down to them before hopping down to guard me himself.

"This is it, Fletch," Perkins said. "The Yuma survivor colony. Four hundred and five strong souls."

He stepped toward me and grabbed my jaw, twisting my face so I was looking at a line of the people he had brought north. They all looked worse for wear. Weary. Bitter. And something more ominous.

Angry.

It was a quiet hate that simmered in the stares they leveled at me. I represented something to loathe. Or something they'd been conditioned to loathe.

"Most of them walked," Perkins said, shifting my view to gaze over more of his people as they gathered to stare at me. "We didn't have enough fuel or trucks to carry everyone. So they walked. Do you know how far it is from Yuma to this very spot? Do you?"

My eyes angled toward him.

"A long way," he said without specifying further. "But they made it. Do you know why?"

He gripped my chin tighter and shook my head for me.

"They persevered, they crossed deserts, and mountains, and rivers, all because they wanted to see the chosen ones," Perkins said. "They wanted to see the ones who'd been favored with supplies, and seeds, and equipment, and doctors, and all the things we were all promised when they shipped us out of Skagway. Do you remember Skagway, Fletch? Do you? That place the government took us to after KIDNAPPING US?!"

He tossed my face aside as he shouted, stepping back.

"You were the favored ones!" he yelled, stabbing a finger toward me. "You received the shipments, the supplies!"

"You turned against us, Perkins," I countered. "You allied yourself with the Unified Government."

"I had no choice!" he shouted. "They had supplies, all your side had was empty promises!"

Unintentionally, a monster had been created. While Bandon was easy to resupply, Yuma, far inland, was not. Possibly there had been delays, even a full disruption of getting needed materials to the survivor colony that Perkins led. More likely, though, I imagined that the man was primed to react to the most minor slight, however unintentional. Siding with Weatherly and the authoritarian message of the Unified Government would not have been a stretch for him, and that he had done, by his own admission, in response to a radio call from us years ago.

"This is what happens, Fletch, when promises are not kept to people who will die without what is promised," he said. "By God, though, I kept them going. I led them. I let them know there were fertile fields and clean water at the end of the journey. All they'd have to do is help me take it for them."

Take...

There was no surprise in his characterization of the mission he'd set for himself, and his people. But there was a moment of shock when I saw who approached him next.

"Fletch, I believe you two know each other," Perkins said as the young woman stopped next to him and put an arm around his shoulders.

"Hello, Fletch," Sheryl Quincy said.

Private Sheryl Quincy. The turncoat uncovered by Martin during the Unified Government siege of Bandon. She'd been traded for Neil, and was on Weatherly's chopper flying away from the exchange point when my friend had been gunned down by Ty Olin.

Sheryl Quincy...

She had connected with Perkins. In more way than one, I realized, as he slid his hand around her and let it rest low on her hip. They were a couple, it appeared.

"You weren't with Weatherly," I said.

"At that fiasco of a battle on the river?" Quincy scoffed. "The man had gotten obsessed with you all. With conquering you. Bringing you into the Unified Government fold. He wasn't thinking right."

"Obsessed, you say."

I spoke the words while looking directly at Perkins.

"Au contraire," Perkins said. "There's a difference between obsession and determination."

"Right," Quincy said, sidling up closer to Perkins. "We're just determined to get rid of you and take what you have. Classic pillaging."

She didn't appear insane. Neither did Perkins. That wasn't a prerequisite for murderous dictators, I knew.

"Why not just kill me, Perkins?"

"Fletch, I don't care if any of you are dead or alive," he said. "You can all scatter into the wilderness. But my people will know the life that you all have enjoyed. It's our time. Yours is over."

If it was more complicated than a bully wanting another's lunch money because they had none themselves, I didn't know. Perkins, for all his faults, was not letting the grandiosity of his self-awareness flavor or cloud the simplicity of his mission—to make what was ours, his.

"Again, Perkins, I'm going to caution you," I said.

"Oh, please do, Fletch."

"Yes," Sheryl agreed. "Heap that caution on us."

She'd been such a demur young woman when portraying a soldier in Schiavo's garrison. It had been a supremely convincing performance. Only Martin's ingenuity and tenacity had brought her treachery into the open.

"Sheryl," I said. "You, better than most, would understand why four hundred people who've been marched across the country to the point of exhaustion will have no chance against a military force, and a population, who've been hardened by numerous battles. Bandon has fought for its survival before. It will do so again, if necessary."

Both Perkins and Sheryl listened to my statement of certainty, smiling as I spoke. That reaction, particularly its uncharacteristic quietness, unnerved me.

"Do you want to be the first lady of Bandon, Sheryl?" Perkins asked her.

"More than anything!"

She grabbed his face and planted a long kiss upon his lips. When she'd finished, they both looked to me again. Though unsettled, I wasn't going to let them get some mental upper hand in the exchange.

"If she's your secret weapon, Perkins, you've miscalculated," I said.

He feigned shock, looking between Sheryl and me, mouth gaping dramatically.

"Her?" he said, pointing, a sour expression plastered on his face. "You think she's my secret weapon?"

Sheryl held it in as long as she could, then she doubled over, laughing, clutching her stomach.

"Oh, this is comedy gold!" Sheryl howled. "Oh, it hurts I'm laughing so hard!"

Perkins, though, didn't break out in uproarious laughter. He simply grinned and fixed his gaze on me.

"I think it's time we show our guest to his accommodations," Perkins said.

Bryce and the two who'd joined him pulled me away from the flatbed as Sheryl continued to laugh, muttering something between the chortles about wanting to see my face when I found out.

When I found out what?

I was no longer just unnerved. Curiosity had crept into what I was feeling. And confusion. Just what sort of secret weapon could Perkins be speaking of? What did he have that could help him take over the whole of Bandon?

And why would the precise nature of it be such a surprise to me?

Forty Three

I was being taken to prison.

Or the version of it that Perkins and his followers had managed to construct in an old bank building, the cell block in the space where safe deposit boxes used to be secured. The vault door, which at one time had sealed the area against intrusion, had been cut away, maybe in some attempt at robbery as the blight raged. Now it lay on the floor, ten tons of useless steel on which a single guard had built a small fire to warm a cup of water.

"New prisoner?" the guard asked as Bryce and the others brought me in. "The one Earl was talking about?"

Bryce stopped, keeping hold of me, and nodded for the others to leave as he glared at the guard.

"Don't ever call him that, Jake" Bryce warned. "Especially if he's around to hear."

The guard shrank slightly at the bigger man's admonishment, nodding an apology.

"The one Mr. Perkins was talking about today?"

"Yeah," Bryce confirmed. "Let's get him squared away."

"Does he know—"

"Shut up, Jake," Bryce cut Jake off. "We just put him in the cell and let happen whatever happens."

Jake nodded and joined Bryce as they led me toward the cells.

* * *

There was no light in the space, save a single candle on a metal stool that rested in the wide aisle between two welded steel cages, one of which had its door open. It reminded me of the cells we'd been placed in by Moto's people in Cheyenne, though there was no stench of blood nor sounds of cannibalistic suffering here.

"Cover him," Bryce said.

Jake took a position to the left and leveled a sawed-off coach gun at me, its side by side barrels looking large enough to crawl into.

"I'm going to cut this rope away," Bryce said, leaning close to my left ear. "If you try anything, Jake's gonna give you both barrels. You got that?"

"I got that," I said.

I wasn't going to try anything. Not yet. Perkins had some sort of plan for me, it seemed clear. One that had to have been hatched when he learned that we would be scouting in his area. That didn't give him or his people much time to prepare a welcome or formulate what it was I'd be useful for, but something had presented itself. Something where my presence would bear some fruit.

My secret weapon...

There was no indication what that was, though it brought much joy to Perkins and Sheryl. Whatever it was, my being there had given some added importance to it—for reasons I could not imagine.

"Hold still," Bryce said.

He pulled at the rope binding my hands and looped around my neck and slid a knife between it and my skin.

"We call that the angel's wing," Jake said. "Makes you look like an angel when you're all trussed up."

"Jake..."

The guard quieted and Bryce finished removing the ropes, then shoved me into the back of the cage. He swung the door shut and took a pair of locks and chains from a nearby hook, using both to secure the cell. A quick tug on the door convinced him that I wasn't getting out. That no one was getting out.

"You both have a good night," Bryce said.

Both?

He nodded toward the entrance, then followed Jake out, leaving me...alone?

I lowered myself to the floor and looked across the aisle to the other cage. It was chained the same as mine.

Someone was in there.

"Hello," I said.

I slid across the concrete floor until I was close to the door, thick steel bars just two inches apart allowing a fair view toward the other cell.

"Hey," I called again, keeping my voice low.

I received no response. Then, I listened, turning my face so that one ear was pointed toward the other cell.

Breathing...

I heard that. It was wet and thick, and shallow, the sound of someone who was sick. In the grip of pneumonia, maybe, I thought.

"Are you awake?" I asked. "My name is Eric Fletcher. Who are you?"

The breathing changed slightly, some voice coming into it now, a small flourish of...weeping?

"Who are you?" I asked.

The sudden bout of crying, as soft as the breathing, ended as quickly as it had started. I turned again, looking into the cell, straining to see through the darkness that was cut only by the flickering yellow candle flame. As I did, and as my eyes adjusted to the low light, I began to be able to make out a shape. A human form, lying on the floor at the back of the opposite cell.

"I can see you," I said.

It might have been a woman, but I thought it was a man. No features were discernible, though the figure appeared to be facing the cell door at an angle. The shadowy form seemed gaunt to me. That state was, or had been, a common trait among those who'd survived the initial onslaught of the blight.

But we were years past that. The person, the *man*, in the cell across from me looked worse than the population of Yuma who'd hoofed it from that desert town to this spot in the Pacific Northwest. He sounded sick and looked starved.

Tortured...

That possibility came to me. It probably was a thought which should have come quicker. A man like Perkins was easily capable of inflicting terrible treatment on a prisoner.

But why? And who was it who the dictatorial leader had imprisoned?

"Talk to me," I said. "Please."

"Life..."

I heard the word, almost a whisper. But not a whisper. Just weak. A man's voice. A...

No...

The figure in the cell began to move, crawling slowly across the floor toward the door until one hand gripped the lowest steel bar.

"Life's tough..."

Dear God...

The hand gripped the bar and pulled, hauling the rest of the man's body to the edge of the cage.

"Life's tough, Fletch..."

The man put his face right up to the bars and looked at me. My friend looked at me.

"Be tougher," I said.

My friend Neil, who could not be there, flashed a smile of sallow teeth and nodded. He'd died. Before my very eyes. And yet he was here, talking to me. How was that possible?

"Tougher," Neil said.

I fell back against the side of my cage and stared across the narrow gap between my oldest, dearest friend and me, and it was I who began to weep this time.

Thank You

I hope you enjoyed *The Signal*. Please look for other books in *The Bugging Out Series*.

About The Author

Noah Mann lives in the West and has been involved in personal survival and disaster preparedness for more than two decades. He has extensive training in firearms, as well as urban and wilderness Search & Rescue operations, including tracking and the application of technology in victim searches.